Four
Resurrection

JOHN GLASS

ISBN: 978-1-914173-00-4

Lp

www.lifepublications.org.uk

Dedication

To my two wonderful sisters,

Alison and Susan.

Acknowledgements

I am incredibly grateful and indebted to Adina Haram for her tireless editing and proof-reading and for her very helpful input during the entire process. Grateful thanks also to David and Jan Holdaway, as always, for their assistance in the publication of the manuscript.

Paddington 2010

There's no doubt about it, I'm being followed, said Jack to himself. He had first noticed the black Audi A5 earlier in the afternoon. He had seen it in his rear view mirror when he had looked to see if it was safe to overtake a broken down car on the main arterial road he was travelling on into Gloucester. When he later indicated to move left into a minor road, he noticed that the Audi also had made a similar manoeuvre. *Nothing strange about that*, he thought at first. But when he had pulled over to the side of the road to check the address of his destination on a slip of paper, he noticed that the same vehicle had also drawn into the curb some metres behind him and as he had later moved away, so did the Audi.

It was four years since his wife, Celia, had been killed in a traffic accident in Estonia. It had been caused by an SUV, driven by a member of a criminal gang whose organisation had been involved in a huge people-trafficking operation. A passenger in the SUV, a young woman who was being exploited by the group, had been badly injured but had survived. She had been heavily pregnant and had subsequently lost her child. As a result of her testimony, Elena, with encouragement and support from Jack, had been given a new identity, as 'Sasha' and had been moved to the UK. Leading members of the gang had been captured and given long prison sentences, something that had resulted in a great 'loss of face' for the organisation. To redress this, the cartel had put a contract out on Jack's life. An attempt to liquidate him had been prevented and the police had intercepted the assailant and the threat to him had been neutralised -

at least for the present. Nevertheless, Jack's sensitivity to his personal security had been greatly heightened, and whereas a member of the general public may not have picked up on the current surveillance he appeared to be under, Jack was acutely aware of the potential threat.

Prior to Celia's death, he had become greatly impacted by his wife's Christian faith and had thrown all of his energy into setting up a charity to help those who had become the victims of people trafficking - especially those whose lives had become scarred through its tentacles that reached into the sex trade. 'Celia Centres' had now been established in Glasgow, London, Birmingham and Manchester. Jack had recently installed two of his closest friends, Damian and Sue Clarke, to oversee the Manchester development but had now asked them to move to the Cotswolds to oversee a new phase in the charity's expansion. So much had been accomplished in just a few short years. Although much of the capital that had been needed had accrued from money made available from the sale of Jack's father's shipping supply business at the point of his inheriting it, there was always the danger of financially over extending. Certainly he could not have got this far without the expertise of another friend and colleague, Simon Bellenger. Simon had been with him almost from the start and it was he that now oversaw the Scottish side of the charity and was based at the Celia Centre in Glasgow. After Gloucester had been put on a firm footing there would be no further plans to expand - at least in the medium term. The next few years had been viewed as an opportunity to consolidate and strengthen everything that they had already established.

So, what to do about this situation? He had tried to get a glimpse of the driver but had not been able to do so, as the person following was keeping just far enough behind to ensure that their features remained indistinct. From the little he was able to make out, the driver seemed to be wearing some kind of head covering - a baseball cap or something similar. However, all appeared to be well, for by the time he had reached his hotel, it seemed that Jack had managed to shake off his pursuer.

The following day he visited the Gloucester Centre. He was aware that his friend Damian would not be there and so used the visit to touch base with a number of the staff. His aim was to address some of the concerns, and understandable teething troubles that had arisen, before setting off to his next appointment, which was to be just nine miles away in Cheltenham.

Jack entered the car park from the main building, looked over to where his vehicle was, and out of the corner of his eye, saw to his amazement, that the same black Audi A5 that had previously been following him was parked on the main road. It had been positioned at a convenient vantage point for the driver to observe anyone entering or leaving the facility. Whoever it was, was looking directly at the gate, looking for his car, and not at the door from which he had just emerged. He was confident therefore, that he had not yet been noticed by the driver.

Edging back slowly into the lobby, he enquired of the receptionist if there was any other exit from the building. He was informed that there was a service entrance at the rear, but the only way out from the car park for a vehicle was through the main gate. Jack took the door that the woman had alluded to, and once outside, tried to take stock of the situation. He could not approach the stationary car from the main gate, as he would be seen. However, to the side of the Centre was a low wooden fence surrounded by bushes. If he could negotiate his way through that, he would emerge about fifty metres to the rear of the Audi.

Getting over the fence would not prove to be a challenge. What was more important was being able to approach the car without his movements being picked up via the driver's mirrors. However, he could not see how that should be an obstacle, given that the driver's eyes would be forward to the gate and not expecting anyone approaching from the rear.

He was now ten metres away and became aware for the first time that the rear and side windows were tinted - something that was both positive and negative. He could not see in, but at the same time, the person driving would not see him either, until he was parallel with the front door. He was just level with the rear door, when to his horror, the ringtone of his iPhone burst into life. In the next ten seconds, seven things happened simultaneously. The driver was alerted, eyes were focused on the side mirror, Jack was recognised, the gears were engaged, the car lurched forward, a black baseball cap slid sideways revealing the head, though not the face, of a woman with short blonde hair.

The phone still continued to ring as the car sped away into the distance. Jack frustratingly punched the receive button with a little more pressure than may have been necessary and saw a name on the caller ID that he had never expected to see again as long as he lived. It displayed the name: Markus Poska.

He had never known the precise designation and rank that Poska had within the Estonian Secret Service - or even if that was the correct designation of the organisation that he was part of. What he was sure about however, was that he was a man of considerable power and influence and who had been instrumental in the operation that had brought, not only the people-trafficking gang to justice, but which had uncovered the activities of several corrupt police officers and put them behind bars.

"Mr Troughton is that you?"

"Yes, Mr Poska, how are you?"

"I am well, thank you. Is this a convenient time to speak?"

"I can't think of a more inconvenient time," said Jack.

"I am sorry, I can call you back."

"No," interrupted Jack, "please go on. It's too complicated to explain right now. So how can I help you? Are you phoning from Estonia?"

"Yes I am but I will be in London in two days time and I would like us to meet up. I know this is a big request as I do not know how your schedule is and I believe you live a long way from London but I cannot impress upon you enough how important it is that we endeavour to connect."

able to later gain entry to the lounge, as they will not be in possession of a First Class ticket."

Jack realised that Poska had thought of everything and two days later Poska rose to extend his hand as Jack entered the lounge having followed his instructions.

"Mr Troughton."

"Please call me Jack - no need for formalities as far as I am concerned."

"And the same for me too," said Poska smiling warmly. "Markus will do just fine."

"Well first of all," began Poska. "Tell me how you have been doing since I saw you last. But before you begin, were there any indications that you were followed this morning?"

"Not as far as I was aware but you are much more adept at these kind of things than I am Markus. Perhaps I may have been for all I know - but at least this place is secure enough it seems."

"And what about Elena - or should I call her Sasha? - Do you ever hear from her?"

"I think 'Elena' will do. You probably heard that I was the one who inadvertently broke her cover in front of some friends. I had not seen her for quite some time and it was a kind of reflex action I suppose."

"There was no harm done. She is no longer a target. Have you seen her recently, however?"

"No, not recently. We did have dinner a couple of times but nothing materialised romantically, if that is what you mean. I know a few years have passed but I just can't get Celia out of my system. I am not sure that I ever will. I know people move on from bereavement, and I am glad for them if they do, but for me it's not something that I have ever been able to do. 'It is what it is' as they say."

One Week Earlier

The snow had changed its consistency. At first it had fallen in tiny flakes on the cars snaking their slow progress along the A417 between Cirencester and Birdlip hill. Now, as Damian peered upwards through the front window of his car to the leaden sky, the wind was hurling snow the size of white feathers against the screen. Had the road been clear he would still be an hour from home. This evening, at the rate the traffic was moving, it was going to be a lot longer - and very much longer if the route eventually became impassible. The long descent from Birdlip towards the M5 was notorious in such weather, but whatever happened, the promise to his wife that he would be home for dinner at seven was clearly not going to be kept.

It was shortly after 8 p.m. before he could get a signal strong enough to connect to his home landline. After the handset was picked up he heard his wife's voice. "Hi Damian, are you OK? I guessed you would be delayed. Is it terribly bad where you are?"

"I'm fine Sue," Damian reassured her. "I just wanted you to know where I was. I am still about thirty minutes away and I am sorry I didn't make dinner."

There was a pause at the other end and then, dropping her voice to just a whisper, his wife continued. "Your meal has been eaten by our visitor. I can't explain now. I will tell you when you get here. I can't speak any louder as she may over-hear me." And then raising her voice to her normal level, and clearly for the benefit of another listener within earshot, continued with slightly more emphasis than was necessary. "Oh I am really delighted that you are OK Damian, I'll expect you in about half an hour then dear. Drive safely."

"Our visitor? What visitor? What on earth is Sue talking about? We weren't expecting anyone. What can she mean?" muttered Damian to himself as the snowflakes fast assaulted the windscreen.

They had only recently moved to the small Cotswold village where they now lived and it was with some relief that Damian pulled his car from the country lane on which their cottage was situated onto his drive. The deluge had abated but it was still with a degree of uncertainty that he negotiated his front wheels through the thick blanket of snow in front of him. He let out a sigh as he applied the hand brake and noticed the car that was standing adjacent to his wife's vehicle.

" Who could this possibly be?" he thought to himself, as he slipped off his wet shoes in the hallway and exchanged them for some loafers that lay by the door.

"This is Priscilla," said Sue, gesturing across to a woman who appeared to be in her late thirties and who was sitting looking entirely at home on their sofa across from the log fire.

Damian greeted her with a smile and thought that the woman looked like a clone of Princess Diana - even to the coy smile.

"I'm dreadfully sorry to impose on you like this," the woman began. But before she could continue, Sue, seeking to spare the *guest* of her explanation, interjected with, "Priscilla was having trouble negotiating the snow and was terrified she was going to be stranded. She saw our lights on and…"

"Well I asked if I could stay. That's the long and short of it, "interrupted the visitor. "I know it's a frightfully odd thing to do - just turn up on someone's doorstep and ask for a bed for the night, especially in this day and age - but I really did not know what else to do. I knew the car would be grinding to a standstill at some point - and well your house looked so lovely and inviting - the yellow light streaming through the windows and so forth - so I rang the bell."

Damian was still standing as he did his best to take everything in. The woman was right, it was odd, but he supposed, what else could she have done? Then, as if anticipating his next thought, the stranger continued.

"I don't have a phone and anyway, if I did, no one would be able to get out to me, the roads being in the state in which they are in. Your wife said that you had a spare room and the bed was made up and that it would not be a problem but if you…"

"No it's absolutely fine. It's not a problem at all," said Damian, reaching down to where she was sitting and shaking her hand before easing himself into an armchair.

"So tell us a little about yourself. Do you live far from here? Were you setting off on your journey or returning home?"

Damian realised that what he was asking could be taken as some kind of 'test of authenticity' but after all they *had* invited a total stranger into their home. It was only fair to ensure that they were not being 'taken in' by a woman that they had taken in.

The woman did not seem to be interpreting his questions as in the slightest way intrusive - which in itself Damian seemed to take as reassuring - and went on to say that she lived in a village outside Oxford, was divorced, had a daughter at university and worked as the head of a marketing and branding company. Then, as if making a decision to move the focus away from herself, she looked at the array of cards displayed on the oak beam set in the stone above the inglenook fireplace and said, "So whose birthday is it? I guess looking at the feminine designs it must be yours Sue."

"Yes, it was mine on 27th February but we generally keep them up for a week."

"Oh, almost the same day as mine," Priscilla replied. Just three days difference.

They talked on until around 10 p.m. And then, having watched the news headlines, they had a light supper. Once they had finished, Priscilla asked if she might retire for the night, so Sue showed her to her room.

The following morning Damian left early for the office and received a phone call from Sue at around 10 a.m. to say that their guest, having not come down for breakfast, Sue had felt it right to tap the door to see if she was OK. Having received a reply that she had a headache, Sue had taken some tablets to the room together with a glass of water. However, Priscilla had only opened the door wide enough to retrieve the painkillers and the drink and had then promptly closed it saying, that if Sue did not mind, she would like to stay in bed a little longer.

At one in the afternoon Sue had phoned Damian again to say that she was worried that something appeared to be very odd and asked what he thought she should do. Damian said that he would phone in an hour to see if the woman had materialised from the room and if not, he would head back home immediately and help to sort the matter out.

At shortly before 2 p.m. the home phone rang.

"Is she still in her room?" Damian asked as Sue answered on the first ring.

"Yes, and I'm really concerned."

"Well," continued Damian, "I've just contacted the local police station, without giving them all the details and asked what our legal position is in a situation like this. We are obviously not going to force her to go if she is unwell but my concern was where we stood if she is emotionally disturbed or something like that."

"What did the police say?"

"The sergeant on the desk asked if, when the woman came to the house, she had forced her way in. I said that she hadn't and he said, in that case, she was our guest as we had invited her in. The police could only get involved if an offence had been caused - you know, if she had become violent or something. When I questioned him further, he said that if someone's mother-in-law overstayed their welcome at Christmas, they could hardly call the police to get her to leave."

"But she's not related to us. We had never even seen her before last night," remonstrated Sue. "Hang on a minute!" Sue dropped her voice to a whisper and brought the handset closer to her face. "I think I can hear someone coming downstairs. Damian! What should I do?"

"Just stay on the line, I'm sure everything will be fine," answered Damian, with rather more confidence than he felt.

"Damian, you won't believe this!"

"What?"

"She has just gone out of the front door and I can see her getting into her car. Shall I go after her and see what is happening?"

"No stay where you are Sue. Something obviously very strange is happening. If you confront her, goodness knows how she might react. Keep on the phone and see if she pulls out of the drive."

"Yes, she has. Why on earth wouldn't she say goodbye... and just go off like that?"

"Don't worry about that. Just ensure all the doors are locked. Then go and check the room she was in. I am setting off for home right now."

Forty minutes later as Damian swung his car into the drive, he found Sue standing at the front door waiting for him

"You'll never believe this," she began, "the woman has been through your entire study."

"You're joking?" Damian said, excusing himself as he pushed past his wife and made his way towards his room.

As he entered it was quite clear that the study had been disturbed. Drawers had been opened and files and personal effects had been rummaged through. He checked to see if the safe had been tampered with and was relieved to see that it had not. He looked in drawers where passports and spare credit cards were kept and nothing appeared to be missing. He touched the track pad on his desktop computer and the large screen immediately came to life, which meant that he had not shut it down the night before but just let it go into sleep mode. He clicked on to the history tab in the web browser and to his dismay saw that during the night someone had been into his email account. "What on earth was this woman looking for?" he asked himself.

"Do you think we should contact the police?" asked Sue.

"And tell them what? That someone we invited in has now left but we think that, though nothing appears to be missing, we believe that they might have rummaged through some of our belongings. How is that going to help? I bet neither of us thought to note the registration plate of her car. We don't know her surname or even that the name Priscilla is genuine. In short, we know nothing about her at all."

"Well, there is one thing but I don't know how it will help us. I found this on the floor when I was stripping the bed," said Sue, producing a mobile phone. "It won't help us of course because it's password protected. What I can't understand, apart from the real reason why she was here in the first place, is why she said she had no mobile phone and why she did not just leave in the middle of the night.

"That's because she knew she would have triggered the house alarm. She seemed to know what she was doing and would have noticed that the security sensors covered just the ground floor. This left her all the time she needed to find my upstairs study and rummage through it," said Damian.

"So why not come down for breakfast?"

"Probably because she did not want to have me ask her any more questions about her background or to ask her when she would be leaving. She would also have seen though her bedroom window that the thaw had begun and that I would be setting out for work."

"But that still does not explain why she did not come down either for breakfast or lunch or why she concocted a story about feeling unwell," offered Sue. "Unless of course," she concluded, "I might leave the house to go shopping, thus giving her cart-blanche to roam around the house at will. But she must have known that would be hardly likely to happen. Not least because I could have easily gone into your study during the morning, discovered that things had been disturbed, and subsequently confronted her while she was here. It does not make sense at all. In fact it's quite unsettling to think that someone we invited into our home in good faith, harboured a malign intent - even if it did not result in violence."

Revelation at the Station

Jack had followed all of Poska's instructions to the letter and the two of them sat opposite one another in the First Class lounge at Paddington Station.

Poska responded to the vibration on his phone, looked across to Jack while at the same time pointing to his handset as if in apology, and took the call.

"Ok send him in," was all that Jack heard before Poska concluded the conversation.

"So you were saying that you had not heard from Elena recently then, is that right?" continued Poska.

"Yes, and you were saying that she is no longer in any danger. But are you therefore implying that I may be?" inquired Jack.

"Well we will come to that in a minute but first of all…"

As Poska was saying this, Damian entered the lounge and greeted a surprised Jack with a wide smile.

"What on earth are you doing here?" asked Jack incredulously.

"He's here at my invitation," said Poska. "I will come to that in a minute. But first of all Damian, bring your friend up to date."

Jack listened to the story of the female intruder in total silence without once interrupting. It was only when the account concluded that he commenced with his questions.

"So you and Sue are OK - you weren't harmed in any way?"

"No, we are fine. A little surprised by the event, but fine."

"Well at least that's something to be thankful for.

And nothing was stolen from your house?"

"Nothing physical," said Damian

"Physical?"

"What I mean is that no items were stolen but she did take information. Unfortunately, I often tend to leave my computer in sleep mode overnight. I once read somewhere that most computer failures occurred at the point they are either switched on or switched off. So that's why I do it. It consumes very little electricity and of course the monitor wakes the moment I move the mouse. She would have had access therefore to my emails and my calendar and I am afraid Jack, all the details of your movements and itinerary. It's terrible to think that I could have put you in danger."

"I wouldn't worry too much about that Damian," assured Poska. "If this woman belongs to the group that I think she does, she would have had the ability to break any basic encryption that most people have on home computers without too much difficulty. And while we are talking about encryption, did you bring the woman's phone with you as I asked? The one she left behind?"

Damian responded by drawing the phone from his inside pocket, passing it towards Poska, and handing it to him.

"Those involved in high level security - governments for example - use almost unbreakable code in their encryption," explained Poska. "Criminal organisations, the Mafia for example, although they are becoming increasingly sophisticated technologically, tend to use burner phones - cheap disposable devices with untraceable sim cards. This woman's phone however, is not of the disposable variety."

Poska turned the phone over in his hand as he continued. "The problem is that Apple do not make it easy for anyone other than the owner of the device to gain access. They do this on the premise that they are protecting their customer - which of course is fair enough. The problem arises at the point that evidence, that could point to criminal activity becomes hidden in its store of data."

"Damian are you sure that there was nothing at all that she conveyed in her conversation that might give us a clue to a possible password?" inquired Jack.

"She told us her name and the area in which she lived, but I don't think for a second that any of that was remotely genuine," Damian responded.

"Well let's take a break for a couple of minutes," said Poska, laying the phone on the coffee table in front of them and signalling to one of his men in the room.

"As this is a First Class lounge there are complimentary refreshments available, and as it's mid morning the options will be tea, coffee and fruit juice together with Danish pastries and fruit. Had we come this afternoon we might have had the choice of sandwiches and Victoria sponge. What would you like gentlemen?"

The orders were made and completed and Damian thought he would direct the conversation a little away from Poska's line of enquiry to something that, though not lighter, was of a more compassionate theme.

"How long has it been now since the accident Jack? It has to be four years... yes it must be," said Damian answering his own question. "The funeral was on the same day as Sue's birthday 27th February. That was 2006 and here we are in March 2010."

Damian sprung to his feet with such speed that Poska's security detail instinctively moved their hands to the inside of their jackets, before they reached the conclusion that the action was not invoking a threat to their boss.

"For goodness sake, what's the matter Damian?" asked Jack, as he watched his friend's reaction.

"We just might be able to work out the code to the woman's phone," said Damian excitedly." When she saw the birthday cards above the inglenook she asked whose birthday it was. When Sue said it was hers, she said that her own was three days later. I don't think that she would have made a thing like that up. She may have just dropped her guard for a moment while she was endeavouring to ingratiate herself with us."

"I'm not with you Damian," said Jack.

"But I am," retorted Poska. "The Apple input is four numbers. Many people use their birthday, and if the woman calling herself

Priscilla did this, we may possibly be able to gain entry. When did you say Sue's birthday was?" asked Poska, lifting the phone from the coffee table.

"27th February," answered Damian.

"So three days later would be 2nd March," said Poska punching in 0203

It did not work.

"But what if a leap year was involved?" suggested Jack.

Poska punched in 0103 with the same negative result.

"Are you sure she said three days later?" asked Poska.

Damian thought for a moment and then admitted, "You know when I think about it, what she said was 'three days different'."

Poska put in 2402 and immediately the phone unlocked.

"The first thing to be aware of, is that it is quite possible, should this woman be a professional, that this phone was left to throw us off the scent," said Poska partly to himself but also for the benefit of his listeners. And as he continued tapping keys and entering menus, added, "She could have dropped the clue about her birthday on purpose. However, the further I go through the phone it appears that it very well may be her personal phone just as we first thought." He turned the screen first to Damian and then to Jack and asked, "Damian, these are the pictures she has taken with the phone and some appear to be Selfies. Is this the woman who you had in your home?"

Damian confirmed that it was and Jack added that, though he was not one hundred per cent sure, it was very possible she was also the person who had been tracking his car.

Turning the screen back to a position where he could see it again, Poska thumbed his way into the 'recent calls' section.

"Well this tells us a great deal. As I suspected she, and by the way she appears not to be Priscilla but Olga, has clear links to Estonia."

"Olga!" exclaimed Damian. "Are you sure? She had a clipped middle class accent. Sue and I actually mentioned that she reminded us of Princess Diana. Olga sounds Russian to me - and how would you conclude that she is connected in some way to the people trafficking organisation?"

"Well first of all," countered Poska, "she could be a typical English rose. But if her family had links to my part of the world, she could easily have been given that name by her parents. This is how she has signed off many of the emails I am running through. I'll need to take the phone away and have our tech people analyse this in more depth. In fact this could be quite a gold mine in terms of our current investigation. As for 'why do I believe she is connected with the problems we have all been caught up in one way or another?' Well that's simple. Many of the calls out of this phone are prefixed with +372, the dialling code for Tallinn. Which brings me to the reason I have called you both here today. What I am about to tell you will most certainly shock you - I'm thinking especially of you Jack - and engender, I am just as confident, a very high level of disbelief."

Jack and Damian instinctively positioned themselves more erectly against the back of the sofa, as if anchoring themselves more securely in anticipation of what was about to be related to them. Poska was not a man to say such things lightly. The world in which he worked was a stranger to the trivial and the inconsequential.

'Do you remember the name 'Escobar', Jack?"

"I most certainly do," Jack responded. "He was one of the main players at the centre of the police corruption scandal. He was among those who interviewed me after Celia's death."

"That's right," Poska continued. "If you remember, we waited some time before we moved in on the perpetrators because we wanted to bring as many of them into the net as possible. There was of course an element of risk in doing that. If we acted too soon we would capture some but run the risk of letting the bigger fish escape. If we delayed too long the whole operation may have been compromised and we could have lost everything. We were fortunate, however. Our timing worked well. In fact very well indeed. It was so thorough, that not only did we detox the police force of a great deal of corruption, but through our monitoring and surveillance, we also unmasked those involved within a number of other professions. There is a saying isn't there that 'money talks'? Well, the paper trails and bank accounts that we have uncovered have spoken very loudly indeed. The results have been deafening in fact. Anyway, back to Escobar. It does not matter what part of the world you are in, corrupt police officers - or 'bent coppers' as I think you call them in the UK - have a very tough time in prison and our country is no different in that respect. Only convicted paedophiles are lower down the food chain. Society is wired in such a way that it seems everyone needs someone to look down on - and that goes for prison too. Escobar has been having a rough time. He's been used to a comfortable life outside with the money he had made and now his world has been turned upside down. The powerful and influential professional has become the impotent and targeted nobody. Obviously, he is one of many in a similar situation and there are some things that the prison authorities are able to do, if they believe an inmate's life is genuinely in danger. But there are limits to what even they can achieve. Long term prisoners have created a powerful network within the system that is a conduit for drugs, information and of course retribution. You have to remember there will be people in there that Escobar would have been responsible for putting behind bars.

One of the tactics that convicted criminals use at times like this, is to offer to bargain information with us in order to make their lives easier inside. This can be anything from implicating fellow prisoners to offering new information. You need to realise that because they are desperate, what they offer can also be either outright lies or have an element of truth that leads to nothing more than dead ends. Anyway, a little while ago Escobar's lawyer said that he had, and I quote him precisely, 'explosive news.'"

Here Poska paused, took a deep breath and looked across at one of the two men facing him.

"Jack, I know that you are going to find this hard to believe but….. Jack, …. he is saying that Celia may still be alive!"

It was as if the oxygen had been sucked out of the room. For what was just a few seconds, but which seemed like an eternity, no one attempted to speak.

Eventually Jack responded.

"But that's impossible. I saw her body in the car Markus. I watched the medics pull a blanket over her face as she was taken to the ambulance."

"It's not just that," interjected Damian. "We all attended her funeral for heaven's sake. What do you mean, she is still alive?"

Poska raised his hands, palms forward, as if halting the advance of a stampede.

"Hold on for a moment. I am not saying that she *is* alive. She may well not be. I am just telling you what Escobar is suggesting."

For a moment all three of them seemed to have forgotten that they were in the First Class lounge at Paddington Station. Although the men immediately around them were Poska's people, a handful of passengers had entered the room since the conversation had commenced and now were glancing across to see where the raised voices were coming from.

Speaking in more measured tones, Poska continued. "We have to take this one stage at a time. Escobar is feeding this story to us piecemeal. He is trying to be clever of course. He is using his knowledge as a bargaining chip, or perhaps several chips in this case. If he tells us everything he says that he knows, he of course has no more power over the situation. He knows this and all he is saying at this stage is that she may still be alive."

"But how can he suggest for a single moment that such a thing could be true?" asked Damian.

"Exactly!" added Jack. "It's impossible."

"Escobar has a number of demands - and even saying this sticks in my craw. A person in my position cannot be seen to be negotiating with a common criminal. Even if what he is saying is true, this is a simple abduction - not a matter of national security."

"What do you mean 'a simple abduction'? This is my wife you are talking about," said Jack.

People were beginning to stare across again and Damian put a hand on his friend's arm, partly in restraint and partly out of compassion.

"Of course I understand that Jack," defended Poska. "It's just that I need you to understand the position I am in. The level of the alleged felony dictates the amount of resources I can legitimately allocate to it. That is all I am saying."

"And what do you mean by 'abducted'?" Jack went on.

"Listen, as I said, there are a number of demands and we don't at this stage know what the others are or how many there are. He has said that he would tell us the basis on which the supposition is being made, and in return, we are to guarantee his safety while in prison. We have told him in order to effect that, it would mean he would have to go into solitary confinement. He argues, and to a degree he is right, that the guards could still get to him if they wanted to."

"So what have you agreed to?" asked Damian.

"We have said that we would move him to another prison and keep the closest watch on him. With this assurance, he told us the following:

He is alleging that the ambulance sped away to the hospital with Elena in it and a smaller vehicle went off towards the mortuary. In the rear of it was a stretcher with Celia's body in the back. In the front was a medic who was driving and next to him was a police officer. It seems that en route to the East Tallinn Centre of Pathology, the vehicle was forced to break suddenly to avoid a dog that had run out into the middle of the road. They pulled into the curb to settle themselves and they say that when they checked to see the gurney was secure, some movement was detected. When they recovered from the shock that the woman they were transporting may still be alive, they both began to take in the consequences. The medic apparently felt responsible for the fact that he had apparently miss-diagnosed the situation and declared the victim dead when she clearly wasn't. The officer, who was one in the employ of the traffickers, realised the implication of someone remaining alive and able to provide a description of the gang member who had caused the accident."

Poska looked across at Jack, who now was bent forward with his head held in his hands which had become curled into fists.

become exponentially complicated. But let me bring you to the end of Escobar's account. The substituted body was admitted to the pathology department and the necessary paperwork completed. They explained the later than anticipated arrival with the story of the dog, which apparently was accepted. You had identified that Celia was your wife at the scene and you had given and signed a statement subsequently. Under Estonian law there is no requirement for family members to identify a body subsequent to death if other corroborating factors have been taken into account. I have known many instances when the next of kin do not want to see the body that had been involved in an accident. Instead, preferring to remember their loved one the way that they had known them and not be haunted by memories of possible disfigurement."

"I can't believe that we all sat through a funeral service and grieved, when all the time, she was alive somewhere. Funeral services are traumatic at the best of times but at least they bring closure. We have no closure now. Her ordeal in these past years, even if she survived them, may have been worse than death. I can't even bring myself to imagine…." said Jack.

"Jack," interposed Poska. "I think you should let me finish before you jump to too many conclusions. Please let me go on. Escobar says she was examined at a clinic. There were lacerations, bruises and abrasions - which one might expect in such an episode - but these were largely superficial and would heal quickly. She had suffered several broken ribs, but while that condition is, as you may know extremely painful, doctors tend not to operate unless ancillary conditions force them to do so - internal bleeding or organ damage for example. Healing takes time but time is all that is usually needed. It seems Celia had been very fortunate. However there was one major concern and that was memory loss."

"You mean she had amnesia?" inquired Jack anxiously.

"Yes, according to Escobar, severe amnesia. I am not a neurologist, obviously, but I know enough about these things to know that there are various types that differ in severity, length and ongoing potential consequences. TGA - transient global amnesia - is more common than people think but lasts just for a few days and there are rarely any long term consequences. It affects only the short term memory."

"Do people get their memory back?" inquired Damian.

"No, I am afraid not. Imagine writing an article on a computer that you did not back up. If your computer fails then the document cannot be retrieved. It was lost because it was never saved. It's like that with a TGA. The sufferer is not saving to short term memory. What they remember prior to the episode usually remains in tact. More serious is TIA, which in effect is a mini-stroke. But Celia apparently had none of these. The accident had left her in a condition where she did not know who she was, where she was, or what had happened. Obviously, the latter part of this diagnosis would have relieved any anxiety that the members of the gang had about potential witness statements or identification."

"Markus, and by the way thank you for being so open and frank with us," said Jack. "You did not have to go to the lengths that you have gone to and I certainly appreciate it. But I can't see why they would want to keep her alive. She was surely a huge liability. The very act of guarding her would itself have been a problem that was surely not worth the effort, given that having her alive was of no advantage to them."

"It seems that they considered her a potential 'bargaining chip' in the event that their activities became exposed," responded Poska. "The thing is Jack, we have not the slightest idea of her current whereabouts or even that she really is actually still alive. You have to remember that."

"If she has total amnesia, does that make her in some way a different person than she was before she lost her memory though?" asked Damian.

"Well, as I have said, I am no expert but my understanding is that people who suffer in this way to the degree that they cannot remember events or even people, retain 'memory' in other areas. They have muscle memory, in that they are able to walk and function physically. Learned skills like driving or riding a bike often still remain even though, when travelling, they may not recognise places that they have visited previously. As far as 'a different person' is concerned, amnesiacs tend to still operate within the moral boundaries that they once operated under. There is of course a major exception to this and that is, if apart from brain trauma there has been brain damage. The potential difficulties in that case are almost endless. I am sorry to have to say this Jack, but physical and psychological difficulties should be expected if such a thing had happened to Celia. However, Escobar has intimated that there was no evidence of that happening as far as he was aware. We may of course have come to the end of the road as far as getting any more information out of Escobar. I have to be frank with you on that. Although of course, we will still try."

"But you have Escobar in prison?" offered Damian.

"Yes we do," agreed Poska. "And under a previous regime in our country there would have been ways to extract all the information that we needed. But thankfully we are living in different times now. I have never believed in the supposition that the 'end justifies the means'. I still don't. If we go down that route, we end up becoming just as bad as the people we are trying to apprehend."

"I understand that," acknowledged Damian. "And I agree, but surely there is more that he knows than he is telling us. I thought you implied that this was just stage one in further negotiations with him."

"My gut feeling is that he has told us the lion's share of what he actually knows already. His personal security appears to have been his main concern and he has got that. Of course I could be wrong but I think that he is just keeping us on a line to elicit more concessions. But we will have to wait and see. Listen guys, we have to be moving off in a moment. I have a symposium to attend on the other side of London but if there are any immediate questions that you have?"

Poska turned to one of his men and whispered something, after which the man immediately left the room and then Poska turned back to Jack and Damian.

"I have a host of things buzzing around in my head like wasps in a nest but I am not sure that you would be able to address most of them at the moment," said Jack. "I think the main issue I would want to know is where we go from here? What plans do you have to take this forward? How should we keep in touch and probably the most important question of all, is how do I go about breaking this to my family, my colleagues and my friends?"

"Well let's deal with the last one first," responded Poska. "It's going to be difficult for you both to hear this, especially you Jack, but I need you both to keep this totally under wraps for now. I know it's going to be hard but if too much gets out, it will have huge potential to impede, if not curtail, our investigations. We still have to look at this little item forensically." At this, Poska again turned the phone around in his hand. "But it seems that there are some people out there who are very interested in finding out how much we know already. The woman who came to your home Damian - Priscilla or Olga or whoever she is, was almost certainly part of that scenario. Needless to say, I would advise you both to step up your own sense of vigilance - something that I believe you will already have taken very much on board. As for keeping in touch, I will leave you with this number. If you remember when we first met those years ago, I said I would not be at the end of the line personally but told you that it is perpetually manned by people who know exactly where I am if the urgency demands it. Also, take it for granted, that if any new developments arise that I think you should be aware of, I will most certainly be in touch."

Poska stood to his feet to signify the conversation was about to conclude and as he did so the men with him rose in unison. At the same moment, the man who had earlier left the room returned, and before joining his colleagues nodded over to his boss.

"I asked one of my men to check out the platform and surrounding area and he has indicated to me that the coast is clear, so we can all be on our way."

Jack and Damian who had also risen, extended their hands to Poska, who shook them warmly.

"In many ways I am sorry to have dropped this on you Jack but of course I felt that you had to know. You can be sure that we will do all that we can to be of help," said Poska

Jack had really come to like this man. His tall, commanding presence always exuded a sense of confidence when he spoke.

"Markus, we really do appreciate all that you have done. You have always been consummately professional and we consider you a friend."

"I am glad that you see things that way Jack. It's good to hear. In fact, we are more than friends. We are actually brothers you know."

"Brothers? What do you mean by that?" asked Jack.

"Oh that's for another time," responded Poska and with that he and his entourage left the lounge.

Olga

St. Petersburg had been known as the Jewel in the Baltic Crown since its founding in 1703 by Peter the Great. Twenty thousand workmen commenced the project from the marshland with none of the machinery that modern construction companies have at their disposal. These were serfs, soldiers, convicts and artisans. Thousands died from famine and exhaustion and it was said that St. Petersburg was a city built on the bones of its builders. In stark contrast, the famous Hermitage Museum is stocked with almost three million of the world's most priceless art treasures and survived both the revolution of 1917 and the ravages of the Second World War.

Two black Mercedes sedans converged from different ends of the city. One made its way down Kamennoostrovskiy Prospect with the historic Peter and Paul Fortress on its right. The other travelled north along the Sadovaya Ulica. Their destination was the Kazan Cathedral. A man emerged from the back seat of each vehicle, their drivers having been told precisely at what time they should return. They pushed past a crowd consisting of both worshippers and tourists, to a pew three rows from the rear of the building. Long experience had taught them that public places were a good environment to meet if they wished to speak in confidence, and of those, sacred spaces were the most suitable.

Both Aleksei Kuznetsov and Diak Sokolov had been involved in criminal activity for as long as they could remember. Kuznetsov had been virtually mentored by his father and older bother. Sokolov had never known his biological family but had grown up in the world of street gangs. Gangs had been a haven to him. Not in the sense of them being a safe place to be but because of the fierce loyalties and fraternal commitment involved. Today both were leaders in their own spheres. The communism under which they had been educated was atheistic to its core. They did not doubt for a moment that their species had evolved over millions of years through a process in which the strong survived and the weak did not. Minnows were the food of larger fish and they, in turn, provided the nutrition for the species that preyed on them - and so it went on up the food chain. Survival of their species depended on them being whale rather than minnow - predator rather than victim. That, as far as they were concerned, was how the world worked. They had no conscience at all about the suffering of the people they trafficked, those sold into sexual slavery, or those ravaged by heroine. Anyway, they rationalised, if they did not do it, someone else would. Had they not taken this route in life, they felt that their future would have been consigned to pushing pens at the behest of some bureaucratic state employer, or even worse, pushing a wheelbarrow on a construction site.

It was natural to talk in whispers when in cathedrals and it was Kuznetsov who was the first to speak.

"Did you ask your man to come back in exactly an hour as we agreed?"

"Yes," answered Sokolov.

"So have you any more information from our people in Estonia?"

"Only to the degree that the cell that was wrecked those years ago and systematically dismantled by the police investigation, allowed our competitors to throw themselves into the vacuum - just as we anticipated. The intelligence that we once were able to extract from the police who were on our payroll, has now all but dried up. All that we are hearing at the moment comes from those who are doing time as a result of that total mess."

"I am aware of all of that. The thing that concerns me is this man Escobar who, probably more than anyone else in that department, has profited from his connections with us. Now, I am told, he is talking his little heart out to make life more comfortable for himself in prison. Our money can buy information and it can hire muscle. What it cannot do is buy loyalty - that's always been our problem. How much do you think he knows?"

"Well he certainly knows Troughton's wife survived the accident but I am not sure if he knows more than that or even if he has passed that information on yet. I suppose that we have to work on the assumption that he will have done. We have people inside the prison and taking him out would not have been a problem. However, I have been told that they have moved him somewhere else, which does not sound good - not because he's out of our reach for a time but because he is now in the pocket of the police rather than in ours."

"Is it right that you tried to take Troughton out when it all kicked off back then? To be straight with you, when I heard of it, I couldn't see the point. Why go to all the trouble - all the potential exposure and risk? He was just some little guy. He couldn't have made any difference to us one way or another if we had left him alone."

"It was about reputation," answered Sokolov. "Can't you see that? We couldn't afford to be seen to be doing nothing. Anyway, the idiot who we sent out to Scotland messed it up and on top of all that, cooperated with the police, to the degree that his evidence proved to be the final nail in the coffin of our operation. The thing is, if Troughton thinks his wife survived, he's definitely going to start poking his nose where he shouldn't. Do you think anyone of our people who have been around his wife could possibly have made contact with him - even if Escobar has kept his mouth shut? That is something we really need to know."

"I'm already on to that," replied Kuznetsov. "I've got someone looking into it."

"Please tell me that this person can be trusted."

"Oh yes there is no problem there. She was born over here but her parents sent her to university somewhere in England. Her father used to work for us."

"What do you mean 'used to work for us?' - people don't just leave of their own accord."

"He was running with us when he was a kid in the Sixties - small stuff at first and then started to climb up the ladder in the same way that the two of us did."

"And so…?"

"And so he got squeamish - got religion or something and wanted out. We told him that he could not just walk away. He knew too much. It was not going to happen."

"And so…?

"And so he got something else."

"What?"

"He got cancer. He was bed-ridden and therefore useless to us in any operational way. There were those who said that if what he had was terminal we should terminate him sooner. However, I thought he could still be of some value."

"How useful could a man with cancer be?" asked Sokolov. "Are you kidding me?"

"Well he was in a lot of pain and needed drugs but had no money for it. His wife was working but that provided just enough to put food on the table, nothing else. His daughter was in the UK and we told her that if she looked after some things for us from time to time, we would ensure that her father got the painkillers that he needed. If she didn't, then he wouldn't. Simple as that."

"And she cooperated?"

"Oh she cooperated alright. She has worked with us for about five years on and off. All she asked was that we did not tell her parents where the money was coming from. They think she has a good job over there and that is how she can afford to do it. Her real name is Olga but over there they call her Priscilla or something? We use her wherever we need a fluent English speaker or someone who knows the British culture. We've flown her all over the place."

"So what has she found out so far?"

"She found it hard to keep track of Troughton. He works between somewhere in England and Scotland. However, one of the people closest to him has recently moved to somewhere they call the Cotswolds - sounds like a tourist place or something - anyway she was going to call at the house on some pretence but changed her tactic when there was some huge snow storm. To cut a long story short, she got them to give her a bed for the night. She got into his computer when they were asleep, got copies of his and Troughton's emails and cleared off the next day. There is some stuff that she has given us that may be helpful in the future but there is no evidence at all that anyone has been in contact with him that knows about the Troughton woman - nothing at all."

"So that's all good then?"

"I am afraid not. She trailed him onto a train to London and saw him go into the First Class lounge and shortly after, the man from whose house she stole the files also went in. It was pointless her trying to enter the lounge as she would be instantly recognised. She thought it was unlikely they would have gone to London to meet with one another, so she concluded that there must be someone else in there that they had arranged to see. After quite some time a man came out that she did not recognise. He scanned the platform like a professional but she was well out of sight. A little while later a group of men emerged together followed by Troughton and another man. She is cleverer than I had given her credit for. The lounge is on platform one and there was a train standing ready to leave in just twelve minutes. She stepped on it and photographed the entire group before alighting from the train before it started moving. Apart from those we are aware of, only one stands out - and here is the bad news - his name is Markus Poska. It was he that must have called the meeting. He is a high ranking officer in the Estonian Secret Service."

Celia 2006

They tell me it is Christmas Day. It seems they had to tell me everything since the very moment I came round in that ward all those months ago. As I write this, I remember that my first conscious memory on opening my eyes, was of extremely bright lights with two figures hovering over me in what appeared to be surgical masks. As my vision adjusted, I realised that I must be in a hospital. Their coats were white and the walls were white and I had some kind of intravenous drip in my arm. They later told me that it was a clinic rather than a hospital and that I should not worry. I think I fell back to sleep or unconsciousness after that. I don't know which. I drifted in and out of that state over the next few days. I had no idea of where I was or even who I was. As the periods of lucidity increased, so did feelings of panic and when that happened, my body, or maybe it was my mind, seemed to push me back under. Perhaps it was some kind of coping mechanism. Anyway I didn't fight it.

In the days that followed, my thinking began to move from dwelling on who I was, to who these people were that were tending me. They were professional enough and if I asked for a drink or for painkillers, they seemed willing enough to comply. But there was no warmth there - no sympathy, no kindness. They were just people 'doing their job'. I would ask them where I was and what had happened to me but they simply did not reply - not even giving me a reason why they were not telling me. Occasionally, other people would enter the room and just look at me. They were not visitors. I often wondered why I did not have visitors. They just seemed to observe me and once they had left the room I could hear the indistinct sounds of their conversations with the staff - obviously talking about me. When they addressed me they spoke in heavily accented English, so it was clear that was not their first language. I knew I was English, because not only did I understand what they were saying, but that was the language in which I thought.

Sometimes, I would pretend to be asleep in the hope of hearing anything being said that would give me a clue to my identity, where I was, what had happened to me and what might be going to happen to me. But they were very careful. They never discussed me in my presence. But there was one exception and that exception was to turn my world, or the little I knew about my world, utterly upside down.

I had retained my usual posture of feigning sleep, when I heard a small rattling sound at the foot of my bed. I knew that was the place where they hung the clip board that contained my notes. I recognised the sound immediately.

"So she continues to improve then?" said a voice, that I assumed came from one of the 'visitors'. They were not speaking English but I seemed to decipher what they were saying - at least most of it. Did this mean that I was bi-lingual? How did I understand the language? Did this mean that I was living abroad? The sense of panic that I had managed to suppress, now began to emerge again. If I was English and abroad this would probably be the reason why I had not had any visitors. If perhaps I had been on holiday, on my own possibly, no one would have had any idea of my whereabouts or even that I had had an accident. I had worked out that I'd had an accident rather than an illness because of the cuts and bruises, and most of all, the excruciating pain in my chest, which kicked in whenever I tried to change my position in the bed.

"Yes sir," a voice said. "As you can see we have removed the drip and she is now on solid food. She still complains of a lot of pain but we are endeavouring to keep that under control as best we can."

"Good, then it's time we had a little chat with her. As you have already been ordered, do not respond to any of her questions, and most importantly, do not initiate any conversation with her unless it directly relates to her condition - levels of discomfort and so forth."

But it was not until they had left the room and entered the corridor that I heard, through a crack in the unclosed door, the whispered words from the 'visitor'. "I suppose she is not aware yet that she is pregnant?"

Those last three words hit me like a thunderbolt and my eyes shot open. In a reflex I tried to raise myself to a sitting position but fell back down again, the pain being too great.

Pregnant? If I was pregnant that means that I was, or had been in a relationship and may well be married. I felt my mind spin - thoughts tumbling over one another like clothes in a tumble drier. And for the first time since this phase of my life began, I felt tears rolling down my cheeks.

It was two days before the 'visitor' reappeared. The 'feigning sleep manoeuvre' had now been discarded. I needed to be awake and alert to everything around me and glean as much information as I could. When my blood pressure and temperature had been taken and the nurse had left the room, two people entered: a man and a woman each dragging a chair from the respective corners of the ward to position them on either side of my bed.

"So how are you feeling today Mrs Edwards?" the man had said.

Mrs Edwards? So that is my name - and I am married! I looked down and noticed however that there was no wedding ring on my left hand.

I remember firing one question after another and the man just letting me reach the end of the list without interrupting me or endeavouring to enlighten me on any of the points that I had raised. He seemed to be the senior of the two, as the woman just stared across at me from the other chair. Her gaze had not moved from my face from the moment he began to speak. She was obviously watching my reactions closely. I remember finding it more than just uncomfortable. It was totally intimidating.

He told me that my name was Tania Edwards and that I had been involved in a car accident in which my husband had died. He said that we were in a place some miles outside of Tallinn - a name that did not mean anything to me. He said that I was at a private clinic. He asked what I could remember about myself and I told him I could remember nothing at all. I noticed that he seemed pleased by that, rather than the reverse, which I found strange. I had asked what my husband's name had been and he had told me that he believed it was Tom. I asked about funeral arrangements, when our respective families had been informed, when would they come and see me and when I would be well enough to return home. I looked across to the woman on my left, and though she continued to remain silent and to stare, her face gave the impression that I had crossed some line and that I was being unreasonable to the point of impudence - even though I was only asking about my own welfare and future. He told me that he was prepared to say nothing more but I should be grateful that they had saved my life and I was getting medical attention. He refused to respond to my question as to who 'they' were, other than to make it clear that they would be controlling my every movement and that I would be able to repay them for their care and attention when the time was right.

It's hard to explain the sense of vulnerability that I felt at that point- the moment when I realised that I was a prisoner. When I said that I would contact the police and that they would help; for the first time the woman's face changed from its formerly blank expression to a dismissive sneer. Her lips changed shape to form a smile but the emotion clearly failed to reach her eyes which now had shifted across to her companion. The words he uttered will stay with me forever.

"You won't be going anywhere in the future without our permission or sanction. You are surely aware of your physical state but will not be aware perhaps of some other information. And that is that you are carrying a child. If you do what we say, and that means everything we say, your baby will be allowed to reach its full term. If you do not do what we say, neither it nor you will survive. If and when the child is born and you fail to totally cooperate with us, the situation still remains. It will be your infant who will be the first to die."

Despite the agony I was in, I lunged forward in the bed. The woman roughly pushed me back down and a nurse was called. The needle that was applied to my arm ensured I lost consciousness within only a matter of seconds.

So now I sit in my small apartment with my baby son sleeping in his cot just a few metres from me. As I write this, I find myself instinctively reacting with the same sense of trauma I felt when the man made those statements all that time ago.

It's a strange existence. I have freedom to move within strictly controlled limits. There is a garden area which amounts to little more than a walled compound. They have allowed me a television which has satellite connection and allows me to see programmes in my own language. I can't say I am re-learning history, for of course, I don't know how much I once knew. I can't watch anything today at all. It is too distressing. No time of year symbolises the importance of family more than Christmas Day. I have long ago realised that my family and friends must assume that I am dead. Certainly if anyone had been looking for me, their search would have entered a cul-de-sac and by now they would have given up. My family would know for sure, that if I had been still alive, I would have already made contact with them to reassure them that I was OK. The fact that I have been unable to do so will have only served to confirm their worst fears.

Apart from my little boy Wesley - I have no idea why I called him that - it has been like living in solitary confinement. Physically I am fully recovered and I have no restriction of movement - a relative and ironic term now I think about it. All I really mean is that I have no medical ailments or stiffness in my muscles or joints. They have allowed me access to a room just around the corridor where there is an exercise bike and treadmill. There is no doubt that whoever is controlling me is involved in criminal activity, why else would I be here? There are staff that clean the room and look in on me. I am quite able to clean my own room, so I assume they are sent in

Jack 2010

One of the hardest things that Jack felt he ever had had to do was to keep the news about Celia from his mother. But the more he turned things over in his mind, he had to ask himself the question, "Was there really any new information at all?" The fact that she may have survived the accident four years ago, did not mean that she was alive now. Perhaps it was better not to fill family and friends with false hope that may only lead to a second phase of bereavement if all hope eventually was dashed. Markus Poska did not seem to be coming up with any new leads and his hunch about Escobar appeared to have been correct. The man was out of information. He had scrabbled around for any thread that might make his life easier in prison but most of it had turned out to be nothing more than bluff or conjecture.

Only Olga's phone had proved more promising. The call log had thrown up not just regular links to Tallinn but also to St. Petersburg, which Poska believed to be interesting. The emails were being examined forensically he had told him - not just for content but for source. One thing was absolutely certain and that was that there was an established link between the people she was working for and the traffickers.

It had also become clear that the group had diversified. Perhaps they had been involved in money laundering and drugs four years ago and that the authorities had been too preoccupied with their focus on the sex industry and police corruption to discover the link. But now there were clear lines of communication, including paper-trails to several other areas of operation that the organisation were involved in.

Now Markus had told him that he was soon to be in London again. This time on a visit with a 'British colleague'. Jack assumed that this was most likely Poska's opposite number in the UK but of course he had not enquired further. He had to visit the London branch of the Celia Centres at some point in the next couple of weeks and so paralleling it with Markus' arrangements should not prove to be too difficult. Markus was meeting his friend at the Carlton Club on St. James Street. The meeting was scheduled to be over by about 7 p.m. and that was when and where they were to meet.

Jack climbed the steps out of Green Park tube station into Piccadilly and then after about a hundred metres, passed the famous Ritz Hotel on his right, before turning right into St. James Street. He arrived at the Carlton Club just as Markus was leaving and saw him shaking hands with the person he assumed to be his colleague, before taking the few short steps down to street level to greet him.

Finding a restaurant in which to have dinner was not difficult in that area and once they had ordered, Jack was anxious to know if there was any more news.

"It's not that we have drawn a blank," said Poska reassuringly. "It's that at the level we are now at, things take time. We want to progress both thoroughly and precisely. To proceed at undue speed may mean missing the one small piece of data that could unlock a whole mine of information. You obvious want to know news about Celia and I understand that. I also do, of course. But I also want to delve deeper. I would not normally be involved at this level as you are aware but we are picking up indications now, not just of international connections, but of people at the heart of government. The political implications are enormous. I can't say more than that, as you will appreciate, but some of the references in the emails we found on the phone, allegedly implicate people at the very highest level."

"So, changing the subject for a moment, what did you mean Markus as we were leaving the lounge in Paddington when we met last, about us being 'brothers'? That was a strange statement to make. So please explain."

"I thought you would ask me that," responded Poska smiling. "I was brought up an atheist. I did have family members that were part of the Orthodox Church but never felt drawn to it personally. People find ritual helpful I suppose and I respected that but it was never anything that attracted me. As I said, I had no real sense of faith, or if I am honest, any sense of a particular need for it.

There were various moments however, that had me thinking about the possibility of a God. One was when I was having a barbecue at my brother's house. The evening was drawing in and the sky was amazing. My little niece ran up to me, climbed onto my knee, hugged my neck with one arm and with the other, pointed upwards to the heavens and said, "Look at the stars uncle Markus, God made them, did you know that? God made everything. Isn't he clever uncle Markus? Don't you think that's wonderful?" I did not want to disillusion her. She was just a kid and would grow up to understand that what she believed was little more than a fairy tale. I was an adult. I had been to university. I lived in the real world and knew that everything commenced with a big bang and everything else emanated from that moment.

When I got home, the conversation with little Anna far from my mind, I went to switch on the TV before retiring for the night. But I could not for the life of me get the remote to work. In my frustration I threw it onto the sofa while saying out loud to myself, "Who the hell designed a thing like this?" Immediately my mind went back to what my niece had said. Did I really believe that the universe had evolved out of a vacuum? If someone was needed to engineer the remote for a remote to exist, did I really believe that one day billions of years ago, nothing collided with nothing in order to create everything perfect in order? And what, or who, had initiated that explosion in the first place - even if there had been one? Did everything not have a first cause? Some time later I picked up a book on Intelligent Design, in which leading scientists had come to the same conclusions, though along a more logical and academic route than my little niece had done. She was expressing simple faith on the basis of something that she had been told. They were using the instrument of their intellect and producing arguments that I was able to connect with. However, that was a far cry from connecting with a God that was 'knowable'. My search, if search it was, seemed to stall at that point.

There were other pointers and markers along the way but signposts are static things aren't they? They direct you along a route but they do not travel with you. I needed a guide not a guideline. And that I found in you?"

"Me?" responded Jack incredulously.

"Yes, when I came to visit you at your office those years ago and we went through those identity photos on the computer. Do you remember that?"

"I remember it happening of course. It would be hard to forget that day. But I am sure I did not say anything particularly significant."

"That's the point though. I wasn't looking for 'arguments' or 'positions'. I glanced at you through the corner of my eye more than once. You had told me that you had a Christian faith, and you know what? I could see it working. After I made a commitment to become a follower of Jesus, someone gave me a copy of 'The problem of pain' by your British author CS Lewis. I had already read another book by him, 'Mere Christianity' and had found a number of the questions I had been grappling with, addressed by what he was saying. One thing, however, that was a real conundrum, was if God was omnipotent why couldn't an all-powerful being prevent suffering? I am sure I am not doing Lewis' argument full justice but it seemed to boil down to the fact that when hurting people find genuine comfort through their personal struggles, it enables them to be credible conduits of comfort to other people who are encountering the same stuff. Do you know what I mean?"

"I know exactly what you mean," said Jack.

"Well I saw that in you. You were not just a signpost you were a fellow-traveller. I hope that as I grow in my faith, God will allow me to be a source of encouragement to others, as you were to me."

"Wow Markus! what a story. And I am incredibly humbled to think that I was able to play a small part in it."

It had been a good evening but Jack was facing an early start the following day. He glanced at his watch and was surprised that it was a little after 10:30 p.m. When Poska noticed him do this, he looked at his watch as well.

"Yes, I think it's time we should be moving on. It's been great to see you Jack, and again, I promise that if there are any fresh developments with regard to Celia, I will most certainly be letting you know."

"Which hotel are you booked in?" asked Jack.

"The Rembrandt."

"That's just a couple of blocks away from Harrods if I remember."

"Yes it's very close by. Where are you staying?"

"The Holiday Inn, Wembley Park," answered Jack.

The two men stepped out of the restaurant in search of a couple of cabs. Usually it did not take too long in that area before one could be waved down. The men had only just gone a matter of a few metres when they noticed two men walking towards them. Both had large muscular frames. When they were just about five metres away, Jack made to pass between them expecting Markus to follow and the two men to step slightly aside to allow them to move past. However, the body language of the approaching men gave no indication that they were about to adjust their posture. Jack sensed Markus drop back his pace and stiffen slightly. At the same time he saw the approaching figure on his left reach inside his jacket. Before the stiletto blade had even became completely visible, Markus stepped in front of Jack extending his right arm as a barrier, thus arresting his forward movement.

"Step back Jack. Keep out of the way!" ordered Poska abruptly.

In one swift movement, he pivoted his body weight to his left leg, at the same time swinging his right foot against the right knee of the man who had drawn the knife. Knees are remarkably flexible joints when they bend in the intended direction. However, they were not intended to operate in reverse. Jack heard the sound of breaking bone almost as soon as he heard the screech of pain. The man hardly had time to drop forward towards the pavement before Poska had regained his equilibrium. The assailant on the right, though stunned by Poska's lightening response, now hurled himself forward - an indication that though the man was strong, he had not been trained to anything like the level that Poska had. Now, all that Poska had to do was to feign slightly to the left and then, at the precise moment the second man was parallel to him his momentum taking him forward, slam his right elbow into the man's kidney. Poska knew of course that this would send the man down but not incapacitate him. The next blow, however, rendered the attacker completely out of action and ensured he posed no further threat. Jack moved towards the knife that was laying centimetres from the first assailant's hand but was stopped by Poska just in time. "The last thing we need are your prints on that weapon," said Poska, drawing Jack away from it.

The whole incident had lasted no more than 45 seconds. Jack could hardly believe the speed with which his companion had moved and opened his mouth to speak but Poska interrupted him.

"Before you ask, I was trained in our equivalent of your SAS long before I rose to the position I now occupy."

"I wasn't going to ask that actually. I was going to question, how you are able to reconcile what you just did with now being a Christian?"

"That is not the slightest problem for me. I trained as a soldier and I remain a soldier. It's just that I don't wear a uniform any more. Anyway, I have a scripture for what I just did," Poska said with a smile."

"And that would be what?" asked Jack skeptically.

"Ecclesiastes nine verse ten"

"So what does that say?" Jack asked, surprised and a little miffed that Poska should know a text that he did not recognise, given that he had been a Christian far longer than Markus had.

"Whatever your hand finds to do, do it with all your might!" responded Poska.

"Somewhat taken out of context I think," answered Jack. "But I'm glad you applied it to this situation nevertheless.

Poska was only half-listening. He was punching something into his phone. It was not 999 but a number that Jack would not have recognised. The last thing that he wanted was the regular police mopping this up. He had no jurisdiction here but the person he had spent time with earlier in the evening would ensure that he would not be troubled by any embarrassing formalities. The people who would be brought in, would be liaising with the officers from the Metropolitan police force but the ensuing investigation would be unlikely to be conducted by the regular constabulary.

Olga 2007

"Kindly take a seat Ms Anapova."

Kuznetsov was positioned behind a large wooden desk, its top inlaid with dark green leather and looked across at her with impressionless eyes.

"So let me first ask you how you are enjoying your work?"

"I am not enjoying my work at all, as I think you know," Olga replied, worrying that she had conveyed marginally more defiance in her voice than she had intended. "You are aware," she continued, "that I would not be doing this at all, were it not for the condition of my father's health."

"Ah yes, your father. I am sorry about that. He grows no stronger but at least we can be grateful that he seems to be maintaining some sort of equilibrium - thanks to the medication that he is receiving and which of course we are paying for. I hear now that your mother has lost her job - such a pity - but at least that means she will have more time to care for her husband. It also means of course, that you are even more dependant upon our good graces, doesn't it?"

There was so much that Olga wanted to say but she knew she would have to operate total self-control. Not to do so would endanger her family and it did not also bear thinking, what would happen to her.

"I am sure you will be wondering why I have asked you to come and see me today."

Olga said nothing.

"We have a little job for you. It will involve some travelling, about 370 kilometres in fact. You will be going to Estonia: to Tallinn to be precise."

"But I don't speak the language. You know that."

"It is not important whether or not you speak the language. As far as day-to-day things are concerned, it is not necessary. The place always has tourists, British, American, Canadian, Australian - so a lot of people understand English. It won't be a problem, I assure you. What we want you to do is spend your time with a British woman who currently resides there and who is enjoying our hospitality."

Olga did not need to be told what this meant and simply waited for Kuznetsov to continue.

"Let me give you a little background. This woman is called Tania Edwards. She was born in England but suffered a road accident in which she lost her memory. She has no knowledge at all of her identity prior to the sad event. Tragically, her husband died in the crash. This was when we, shall we say, 'brought her under our auspices'."

Olga inwardly cringed at the sickly smile she was witnessing.

"Yes, under our auspices - our wings if you like - she was not aware that she was pregnant. She now has a child - a boy that is just a few months old. We are impressed by the skills that she has. She is doing a very good job as a translator for us and other secretarial duties. We have also found that she is very adept at handling spreadsheets and this has also been added to her duties."

Olga considered for a moment the sensitivity of the data that this woman would be handling and could use against these people, if ever she passed what she knew on to the authorities. As if anticipating her thoughts, Kuznetsov continued.

"Of course we change all the names and locations in the reports and the captions on the spreadsheets are also false. As soon as she finishes her work it is simply a matter for a 'find and replace' procedure to be done on a word processor for us to insert the correct data. It takes us just a matter of seconds to do. Edwards poses not the slightest threat to us. Her computer is not connected to the internet.

She has no access to a phone or communication with the outside world. And then of course, there is the auxiliary matter of the safety of her son."

Olga felt a cold chill pass over her. This woman was being controlled and manipulated in exactly the same way as she was - though at the moment she enjoyed marginally more freedom.

"So you are wondering where you come into this arrangement Olga I am sure. I may call you Olga, may I?"

Olga again made no reply. This was no more than a rhetorical question. This man was seeking no permission from her for whatever he wanted to do - that was for sure.

"In a nutshell Olga, I want you to befriend her. We believe her memory to be entirely lost in terms of her identity but we cannot be entirely sure. It may well be that she will open up to you. It should not be too difficult to gain her confidence. To put it bluntly, she has no one else in her life to make contact with. She will be drawn to you like a thirsty person to an oasis. Some people would say that the conditions that we have created around her, amounts to 'emotional sensory deprivation' but we would not go as far as that. She does of course have her child - though those conversations must be something of a one-way street I would imagine."

"So what you are asking me to do is to spy on her. Is that it?" said Olga, barely containing her anger and disgust.

Kuznetsov paused for a moment and looked at her over steepled hands before replying.

"Yes, I suppose it would be fair to put it like that. But there is more. We believe that Edwards has a great degree of potential. We think that, not only has she been through university at some point, but that she would be some use to us as an operative in the future. We are asking you to assess that for us. For obvious reasons she does not exactly look upon us warmly and.... well you know what I mean. It may be different... woman to woman shall we say."

"I don't have a great deal of choice do I?" said Olga resignedly.

"Frankly, no you don't and I must offer you a very serious word of warning. You need to be very clear about what I am saying, Olga.

We demand your total loyalty. If you fail to comply with our wishes in any respect, if you fail to pass on what you are have gleaned, if you step out of line to the smallest degree, not only will our support for your father end but you will be severely punished. Are you clear about that Olga? Are you entirely clear?"

Olga nodded.

"I don't need you to nod Ms Anapova. I need you to speak," growled Kuznetsov.

"I'm clear!" responded Olga.

"Good! I am pleased to hear it. Now listen carefully to the arrangements that we have made."

Celia 2007 March

10th March. They told me that the New Year would bring changes but the monotony has been relentless. If I did not have little Wesley I do not know what I would do. I worry that I am virtually the only person that he has contact with. Perhaps it's not so important now but it will be in the future, as I have no idea how long this ordeal is going to last. I have started praying now - not just in the night but as a regular routine. I wish I had a Bible. I must ask for one. They have told me I will shortly have a visitor. I already have regular visits from 'moustache' and 'brown shoes'. I am not interested in having anyone else like that. They refer to this new eventuality as if it was some special event that I would want to embrace. Why, I can't imagine.

They have been giving me spreadsheets to work on. The numbers involved are huge; multiple millions. I am amazed at how easy I have taken to these. I assume that I had these skills before my husband died. I often wonder what he was like - not just what he looked like but the kind of person he was. I wonder if Wesley looks like him. It breaks my heart to think that he never got to see his son. Sometimes, when I am praying, phrases come to mind and I wonder if they are verses from the Bible. I have a deep sense inside that the God I am praying to cares for me but I find it hard to reconcile that awareness with the situation that I am having to endure. I keep on telling myself that it could be worse. At least I am not being physically harmed and Wesley and I have food and shelter. From what I see on the television there are many in the world that do not enjoy that. I have found channels that are devoted to Christian teaching and worship. This is becoming my church I suppose. A phrase keeps coming to my mind.

'The word of God is not bound'. Right at the back of my mind I have the feeling I once knew what that meant but I don't seem to be able to bring anything to the surface. I watched a film the other day, the central character of which was a man called Jack Ryan. It was playing in the background as I was mixing some food for Wesley. I was not really paying attention to the dialogue. I was concentrating on what I was doing. Then the weirdest thing happened. I heard the words: "It's me, Jack, come over here!" and I dropped what I was doing and set out towards the room where the TV was. It was strange, and even as I write this, it sends a shiver down my spine. It was incredibly odd.

24th March. Well, whatever 'new visitor' means, I am going to find out tomorrow. I wonder what he will be like. I must confess to feeling anxious. I have got used to the routine - monotonous though it is. There are no surprises and I have begun to feel safer with the 'known'. It's amazing that only a couple of weeks ago I was thinking of asking for a Bible and a few days later they asked if I would like some reading material. I have mentioned a handful of novels - in English of course - and a Bible. I will have to wait and see if I get them. If they have no problem with me watching television, then they are surely not going to find books a problem.

25th March. She came this afternoon. Yes, I really do mean 'she'. I was not expecting that. To be honest, today has been the most momentous day since I came round after my accident. I find myself shaking even as I write. I don't know what to make of it all. I can never remember being so hopeful, and at the same time being so scared. I will sign my journal off. Please God help me and give me wisdom!

Olga 2007 March 25th

Olga tapped the door of Celia's apartment with a great deal of trepidation. They had told her to befriend this woman and that it should be an easy enough thing to do, given she would be her only adult life-line in the world. *Perhaps this should not be too hard*, she said to herself as she waited. She had agreed to cooperate. How could she not? But the anxiety that she felt was not about the challenge ahead but about the decision that she had reached moments before arriving there. It was something she had been mulling over for days and the implications were huge. She had had no more than four hours sleep the previous night. Nevertheless, she was resolved to proceed with the course she had eventually decided upon.

The door was opened by an attractive woman a few years older than herself. She looked in good general health but her complexion was slightly jaundiced she thought and concluded that would probably have been the result of so much time indoors. She looked past her through a window to a yard area, which meant that she and her baby must have some recourse to at least a modicum of fresh air.

"Good morning. You must be Tania," said Olga extending her hand. "I am Olga. I think you were expecting me?"

There was a look of clear astonishment on Celia's face and her mouth stood open.

"They told me to expect a visitor but I expected it to be a man for some reason." And realising that she had not yet shaken the proffered hand and was keeping this woman standing at the door, ushered her in to the sparsely furnished room.

"Ah so this must be your baby," said Olga as she moved across the room to a cot that stood beside one wall.

Celia instinctively stepped in front her to block her path. No one had ever touched her son, other than herself, since he was born. *Had this woman been sent to take her baby away. Please God, surely not,* thought Celia, her terror showing on her face.

Olga realised immediately that she had been insensitive. This was not a good start. She should have thought this through. Naturally this woman was exceptionally protective of her son.

"I am sorry Tania. I was not going to pick him up; not even to touch him. Please don't be afraid. They told me his name is Wesley, is that right?"

So this woman has been sent from the people who are controlling me. How silly of me, Celia thought to herself. *Why would I imagine that she would be any different to the men. The only thing that was different to the other visitors was that she was the same gender as herself. They had nothing else in common.*

The two women sat facing one another as if weighing each other up and Celia was somewhat disconcerted as to why her visitor appeared to be scanning the place with her eyes and giving particular attention to the corners of the ceiling.

"I am going to be very direct with you," began Olga. "I know we do not know one another at all and that there is absolutely no reason in the world why you should trust me - and actually there is no reason why I should trust you either come to that. What I am about to say to you will have huge implications for my life, and those that I love, should you ever relate a single word to anyone about what I am going to tell you."

Celia felt she was going both hot and cold at the same time. For months she had not had anything approaching an intelligent conversation with another adult and here was this woman, who she had never met before and had been sent by the very people who were holding her captive, inviting her into confidences that, if she broke, may have catastrophic consequences. Was this woman really putting

also committed to finding some solution to Tania's dilemma. But what could two vulnerable people do against such odds? The phrase 'vulnerable women' had first come to mind but she had rejected it. Their vulnerability was not because of their gender but because of their situation. They were not 'damsels in distress', however distressing their situation was.

"At this point Tania, you have to realise that I have no 'plan of action' - no scheme to spring you from this cage. All I really wanted to do today was to meet you and assess whether we really could begin to trust one another. And you know what? I really think we can. What do you think?"

Celia simply didn't have the words, so she just stood up, moved towards Olga and as Olga stood too, they met in the centre of the tiny room and hugged. As they held one another, Olga sensed the rhythm of uncontrollable sobbing emanating from Tania's body, and when she eventually looked up, saw the tears streaming down her cheeks. Olga had never been wired-up for tears. It was not that she was unable to 'feel' - she felt intently. It was just that her upbringing in Russia had impregnated her with a stoicism that made it hard for the emotions that she felt to be shown or to be expressed.

When they resumed their seats, Olga made it clear that she would have to leave before too long. They may not have been able to overhear what had been said but a record would have been made of the time that they had spent together. Had she left too early the assumption would have been that no connection had been made. Were she to stay too long it may have appeared strange.

'This has been amazing," said Celia, once she had composed herself. "It's like a dream. I will have to pinch myself and hope I do not 'wake up'. Never for one moment did I expect to find a friend today - but to discover an ally! What an answer to prayer!"

"Why prayer?" asked Olga.

"Oh, perhaps I didn't tell you - we've both been trying to cover so much detail in such a short time. It's just that I have found myself praying and now it is something I do regularly. I have concluded that Christianity must have been part of my life before all this happened.

In fact, I hope that when I get to eventually open that parcel, that there will be a Bible among the books."

"I told you that my father, and now my mother, became Christians some time ago," responded Olga. "In fact that is one of the reasons my family is in the trouble we are in I suppose."

"How do you mean?" asked Celia.

"Well it's obvious isn't it? I mentioned that in my story.

"You told me in your story that your father was of no use to them after he had become ill but before that you said that he wanted to leave the organisation because of his new faith. But, if I understood you correctly, you implied that if he had not became ill they would have killed him anyway and when he did become unwell they used that to force you to work for them to pay your parent's medical bills."

"I suppose you are right," conceded Olga. "There is no doubt about the transformation I saw in my parents, especially my father. He is a brave man, always was, and knew the risks he would be taking when he knew he had to distance himself from them. He is showing that same courage in his suffering. It is terrible to watch him. At least he does not know that they are controlling me. He thinks that I am having a good time in the UK. I just hope that he never learns the truth. So what day is it today? Ah yes, Sunday. How about we meet at the same time every week? Would that suit you?"

"Of course it would!" responded Celia enthusiastically. "It will be something I shall look forward to. The days will not pass fast enough."

"Yes I know," said Olga. "But we will have to stay focused. These will not just be social visits - even though I will look forward to them too. We have to find a solution to both our problems, as impossible as that may seem right now. It is going to be dangerous and we both know that there is not just the two of us to think about. Keep praying Tania, and while you are doing that, look for every opportunity you can to retrieve even the smallest details of your past from the depths of your mind."

Over the next few weeks the two women grew closer as friends but could not find themselves any closer to a solution. Kuznetsov and Sokolov had asked for progress reports and seemed to be becoming impatient. On the one hand they were pleased to hear that the woman had not recalled anything from her past and they were glad that Olga seemed to be making progress in building a relationship. The problem was that they were not learning a great deal about the areas that the British woman could be of use to them in the future. The expense of flying Olga to and from St. Petersburg was inconsequential - petty cash to them - but time was passing and little progress was being made.

They thought it strange that Olga had made the suggestion that false passports and papers should be created for Edwards and the kid. No one knew that they were at the apartment or even existed. In fact, the British woman was supposed to be dead. But the more they thought about it, the more it made sense. What if the authorities came snooping around, or if there was a raid? How would they explain who these people were? They had agreed and of course it had been simplicity itself to put the documentation together. However, they had also agreed that there was no way those to whom the documents referred, would ever get possession of them.

For her part, Olga was also becoming concerned that she was not passing sufficient information to her controllers - virtually nothing in fact. She was aware that she would not be allowed to maintain contact with Tania unless she could provide data that they would consider useful. The problem was she had no idea how much she had got. She had passed on what Tania had told her about 'discovering prayer'. There was nothing incriminating in that but least it was something. She remembered the scorn and derision with which the news had been received. It was Sokolov who had pulled out his mobile and shouted into the unconnected handset, "Protection! Protection! Double our personal security detail right now - someone is praying!" And then everyone had fallen about laughing.

Celia 2007 May

My visits from Olga continue to be the highlight of my week. The only cloud on the horizon, and it was a dark one, occurred when she told me that her handlers were becoming impatient with the lack of information she was passing on to them about me and that before long the visits may be curtailed or even stopped. She tells me that her mother is now suffering poor health, though her father seems to be remaining stable. Bless her, she has so much to contend with in her own personal life, without burdening herself with my future. She started out by being a huge support to me - just can't say how much that has meant. It has been awesome. However, I am noticing that perhaps, at least in some small ways, I have also been a source of strength to her. I do hope that that is true.

I have been reading my Bible a lot and I was thrilled to find the phrase that had kept coming to my mind 'the word of God is not bound'. It was from the Bible after all. It was when Paul was writing to the young man he was mentoring and I came across it in his second letter to him. Paul, though innocent of any crime, was in prison and was reassuring Timothy that, even though he was physically vulnerable and confined, the power of God through His Word, was both liberated and liberating. I have underlined 2 Timothy 2:9. I am grateful that God gave me that, even before I was sure it came from the Bible - which I suppose again goes to show the truth of the passage.

I am not sure where Olga stands as far as faith is concerned. She has obviously been impacted by the faith of her parents. She has told me so much about them and I would love to meet them - but that's hardly likely to happen. I can't even move out of these four walls.

Other things seem to be resurfacing, most of them meaningless. It's not happening so often that it's leading me to believe that my memory is coming back, but at least I suppose it is a good sign. I shall jot things down here, however incongruous they may appear, just as a means of keeping a record. At the moment they feel like pieces of a jigsaw - strange shapes and not connected. My main problem is that I don't know what the 'picture on the box lid' looks like. If I did, things would be much easier. I told Olga about this and she said that when she used to do jigsaws when she was a girl, it helped to fill in the straight edges first. It provided a framework in which to work. I think I can remember doing that too, but I am not sure how relevant that is in my case. For a start, what are the 'straight edges'? Perhaps they are the things that I can be totally sure about.

I see on the news today that a British girl Madeleine McCann has disappeared from her bed in a holiday apartment in Praia de Luz in Portugal. I am reminded that I am not the only one experiencing the terrors of abduction. Praying for the parents today.

It's now the end of the month and Olga has confirmed, that if next week she does not come up with something worthwhile, from their perspective, they are going to curtail her visits to me. I can't believe it! We will have to seriously talk through our next steps. The problem is we don't seem to have a strategy. Our options are so limited. We will be into June when she comes next week. I think both of us are feeling the pressure but neither of us seem to want to admit it to each other for fear of dragging the other down.

On a positive note, I have been thinking a lot recently about my 'straight edges' and I am surprised how many I have got - my faith in God, my love for my son, my friendship with Olga and my abiding hope that, however uncertain things seem at the moment, I am still believing for a breakthrough.

Six months ago they told me that the apartment I am confined to is outside a place called Tallinn. The name meant absolutely nothing to me at the time but when I think of the name these days my mind conjures up images of a church, a cafe and a man about my own age. Could this possibly be Tom, my husband? I am not sure after what Olga said. Is it really possible that his name was not Tom or even that my name is not Tania? If they are three pieces of the jigsaw puzzle, I certainly can't get them to connect. I have tried them from different angles in my mind but nothing works.

I dreamt a few nights ago, that I was stumbling around in a street as if I was lost. I asked people for directions and no one was able to help me. They kept asking me the same question, "What street are you looking for?" and I could not answer them, so they just walked away each time giving me a similar backward glance, thinking, I suppose that I must be mad. When they were just out of earshot I recalled a name. I shouted after them 'Raekoja Plats' as loud as I could but they could not hear me. They had gone. And then I woke up.

Olga 2007 June

Celia answered the door to her friend and was somewhat confused by the overly bright expression on her face. Today threatened to be the last time they would be able to meet for a month, and here she was; beaming from ear to ear. When they had settled opposite one another with a cup of coffee in their hands, it was Celia who was the first to speak.

"So are you going to let me into the secret?"

"It's not really a secret," said Olga, with the broadest smile. "It's just that I have passed on some information that at last they seemed pleased about. They have not said for sure that they would re-think our arrangement, but I think they might."

"Information?" asked Olga, hesitantly.

"Yes, I told them that I had discovered from you that you had high level intelligence skills that you had utilised in the past and that, though you could not remember from where, I suggested that it could have been that you had spent some time in the police. I was not going to mention the police, for obvious reasons, but it did not appear to put them off. On the contrary, they seemed to warm to the possibility. It's good news, isn't it?"

"Good news!" exclaimed Celia frantically. "It's utter rubbish and you know it is. Why would you even think of telling them something like that? All they have to do is to give me tests of some sort and when I fail them, we will be in a worse position than before. It's a lie Olga and you know it. They have given me things that looked like IQ tests before - completing sequences of numbers, picking out the shapes that don't not fit in a line of options - but they did not even tell me the results. They just took the papers away. Now I'll get something exponentially more complicated and that will not only reflect badly on me Olga, it is sure to also bring your judgment into question."

"You're worrying too much. OK, they might examine you in some way but you will do fine. I'm sure you will. Listen, how long have you been stuck in here? Just think about it. We have to take some risks. We cannot keep doing nothing. Who was it who said that repeating the same process time after time and expecting different results is a sure sign of madness? Whoever they were, I am sure they must be right. This is what I have been thinking - if they take the bait, they may well give you some kind of assignment - the kind of thing that I have been forced to do. That will get you out of these four walls and that increases your options and the chance of getting free from them."

Celia sat back in her chair, her arms folded, and blankly stared past Olga into the distance. She started to think through the options. If they gave her tests and she failed them, what was the worse that could happen? The two of them would probably be in the same position that they would be in now anyway, with their meetings curtailed or stopped. They would surely not punish Olga. She was too valuable an asset to them. They may conclude that her judgment had been wrong but probably assume that she was just trying hard to be helpful. Perhaps there was not too much of a risk after all. Anyway, the matter was out of their hands.

Almost two weeks passed before the Tallinn visitors, 'moustache' and 'brown shoes' came to see her again. They did not mention anything about either tests or exams. What they did inform her of however, was that they were going to introduce her to surveillance techniques - how to follow targets without being noticed and how to shake off a 'tail' should she be the target herself. She could not see any problem with the idea, as at least it would get her out of the apartment for the first time since she had been held there. But her next thought was about Wesley. He would not be able to accompany her; but neither could he be left on his own, even for a couple of hours. The thought filled her with dread. When she expressed her concerns to them they told her that they would arrange for a qualified person to look after the boy and that he would be perfectly safe. The audible sigh of relief that exhaled was followed a little while later by a sharp intake of breath as they told her what qualified as his safety and that, should she try anything stupid such as trying to elude them or contacting any third persons, she may never see him again.

They had allowed Olga's visits to remain weekly and had not stepped them back to monthly intervals as they had once threatened. And when Celia had related the account of their time with her on the next occasion that they met, both felt that they were taking a positive step forward, even though the incremental steps were certainly small.

"Well at least this obviates you being blamed for my failure by taking my 'making the mark' out of the equation," Celia assured her. "If I don't do well, the onus will rest entirely on me or even on their inability to train me well enough."

"Believe me Tania, these are the kind of people who are unlikely to blame themselves for anything. Anyway, did they give you any idea when all this would start? It surprises me that there are such gaps between when and the decisions that they make. I suppose it's because they are trying to be cautious but it does mean that everything just drags on and on."

"Things 'just dragging on' has become part of what I do and who I am, I am afraid Olga. But, changing the subject for a minute, how are your parents?"

"It's certainly a struggle for them. My mother is not well as you know, and apart from carrying her own problems, she constantly worries about my dad. I find it remarkable how long he has lasted. He certainly is a fighter make no mistake. Being out here means that at least I get to see them. They think that I am going to and fro to the UK rather than coming to see you of course. Coming here each week is not justifying my existence as far as the organisation is concerned and so there are an increasing number of other duties they are expecting me to fulfil on top of this. But if it ensures that dad's medical bills are covered, then that is fine with me."

Celia 2007 September

It's September and now thing are really starting to move along, or should I say, accelerating at speed. Wesley has been baby talking for some time and is now walking. I try to do everything in my power to stimulate his imagination but being as confined as this, is so unnatural and it can't be good for him. I have started to pray about this more than anything.

I have been informed that my 'training' is about to start any time now. Apparently Tallinn is so packed with tourists over the summer that the conditions have not been conducive to the kind of things that they want to teach me. I watched a TV programme about cruise ships the other night. It seems that a lot of them dock here as part of their Baltic excursions. They showed the tours that they take the passengers on when they are in port and so many of the places have a vague ring of familiarity about them. But there was nothing that I could say I really recognised. I obviously must have lived and worked in the area at some point and possibly for a reasonable length of time. How else would I be so fluent in the language?

Yesterday was one of the most difficult days of my life. The two visitors arrived bringing with them a woman. I knew this would happen at some point of course but never realised the panic I would feel when the woman walked over to my son. It was not that I felt that she was going to harm him. It was the thought that the two of us would be separated for the first time in our lives. I started to weep and then to sob. I want to retain my dignity before the three of them but I have to admit that I cried out as 'brown shoes' took me roughly by the shoulder and drew me towards the door. I protested that I couldn't go but they insisted that I must. I reached the hallway, and as the door was closed separating me from my boy, I was still looking over their shoulders, as if by some Herculean effort my gaze could somehow assure Wesley that he would be OK. When I reached the outside door my senses were immediately assaulted by a myriad of sights and sounds. The small yard had afforded Wesley and I some fresh air - but this was a whole new atmosphere. Olga would not understand as she had never experienced this but here I was seeing distances that extended far beyond the few metres I had been used to. What Olga would have assessed as being a 'fairly busy street' seemed like huge and milling crowds to me. And the traffic, oh the traffic - speed... noise... commotion... confusion.

They bundled me into the back of a car. 'Brown shoes' drove and 'moustache' stayed next to him in the passenger seat. I could not get Wesley out of my mind. How was he coping without me? Was the woman being kind to him? A few minutes ago I did not want her to touch him, now I was hoping she would be hugging and comforting him.

I did not get much of a chance to think about anything for the rest of the day, apart from the instructions that I was being given. The 'visitors' were professional and precise and for my part, I tried to go along with everything that they asked of me. I shall not write here in my journal all the events of my first day, other than to say that they appeared fairly satisfied that I had got to grips with at least the basics of my first day of initiation.

I just could not wait to get home. It could not have been much more that six hours that I had been away but it had seemed like an absolute eternity. When they unlocked the door of the car so I could get out, I hurried towards the front door. But of course I had no key. I can't ever remember a time when I held a key in my hand but obviously I must have done. After all, I knew that I could drive. I had been in a car when my accident had happened and today, as 'brown shoes' had been driving, I had been anticipating the gears he would move into and the manoeuvres that he would make.

Eventually the door was opened and I raced along the corridor to the room where I had left him. As I entered, I saw my little man sitting on the floor with his toys - I had insisted that they had provided toys for him - and when he saw me, he struggled to his feet and tottered towards me, his face smiling and his arms reaching out to me. The woman, who had been sitting on a chair watching him said nothing. She acknowledged neither him nor I and simply went to join 'moustache' and 'brown shoes' at the door. Before they returned to their car they told me that that this exercise would now be a regular part of my future routine.

I cannot wait to tell Olga about my ordeal the next time I see her. She told me last time she came that our time together would definitely be reduced to once per month now that the training has started. We have become really close as friends but there is one thing that I have always been reticent, almost afraid to ask her - though I plucked up the courage the last time she was here. She has so much more freedom compared to me and can move freely between countries. I could never understand why she did not simply go to the authorities and report, not just what they were doing to her, but pass on information about the organisation's criminal activity. They would have been sure to give her immunity against prosecution. She must have had countless opportunities to do this.

When I eventually raised the subject, I almost wish I hadn't. She said that right at the beginning they had told her that if ever they were arrested, even if she was not directly involved, her parents would be killed. I asked how was that possible if the gang who was controlling her had been taken into custody. She said that they had told her that they sometimes use criminal groups not directly controlled by the organisation - 'hired muscle' I think she called it. She said that they had told her that these people had been held on a 'retainer' and had been instructed to, at a signal from them, kill my mother in front of my father's eyes, so that the last thing he would see before they killed him was the death of his wife. Dear God, to what extent will these people go? In one way, I suppose this should not have surprised me.

When I heard this it answered another question that I had been thinking, almost fantasising about. When I had heard I would be going 'outside' for training I realised that this would mean that I would learn the address of the place I was being held and how to get to and from it. I had dreamt that, if by some miracle I could get Wesley out with me, I could go to the police. When I heard Olga's story I understood that would be completely impossible.

I pray about these things all the time but I have to admit that I feel that, even though I am asking God to help me, my options seem to be fewer and my scope for getting out of here just as narrow as they always have been. Anyway, I was reading in the book of Acts about when Paul was in a ship in a huge storm and they were drifting towards the rocks and it looked like they were all going to die. He stood up and made this big faith declaration by saying in front of everybody, 'I believe God'. When the sailors later took soundings, they found to their horror that they were even nearer to the rocks than before he had spoken. However, even though they went through a terrible time and were shipwrecked, not one single life was lost. Well that encouraged me - at least a bit anyway.

Olga really surprised me the other day when she informed me she had told the people that she has to report to, that they should ensure that I had papers. That was really brave of her. But that now seems to be overtaken by events, as the TV news said that digital ID's have been introduced in the country and that everyone has to have one and be able to produce them whenever they are asked to do so. I suppose if these people are able to counterfeit passports, they will find someway of producing an ID for me. Also, I found out that this year Estonia will be the first country in the world to have electronic voting - not that that is likely to affect me.

I got to thinking the other day that many of the things that I write in this journal are, to say the least, incriminating if ever they should be found. No one has ever asked to search my things - they hardly see me as a security risk - but I am not going to take that chance. I think I will give the jottings I have done thus far to Olga to keep for me. It might be safer. In fact, I think I may stop writing things down like this altogether. It's too dangerous.

A few weeks ago Olga brought one of those floppy rabbits for Wesley. He won't let it out of his sight and takes it everywhere with him, dragging it along beside him by its ears. I feel my eyes welling up sometimes when I watch him. It's become his security blanket.

have suggested to Olga that she also thinks about creating a diary as it might prove a 'release' for her too - but perhaps for different reasons. If ever she was able to extricate herself from her controllers, she would at least be able to log her 'evidence' with far more precision. She said she would think about it.

It must have been about six months ago that they astonished me by saying that I would be supplied with a non-traceable burner phone and believe it or not, an internet connection. They have even installed wifi in my apartment. Of course, they are not stupid. The computer they have made available has software on it that not only records my browsing history, but also virtually every key stroke that I make. They tell me that they are able to remotely monitor when I am on or off line, the sites that I visit and they say that they can change the parameters of my settings remotely. For that reason, I would never consider writing this journal with anything other than pen and paper.

Every so often they remind me about how vulnerable my situation is. This usually happens around the time when I am being granted some form of additional 'freedom'. Giving me access to the web was a case in point.

It was at a time like this on a visit, that they seemed to focus an unusual level of attention on Wesley. They began to make small talk with him - something that they had never done before. They even ruffled his hair as they got up to leave. I noticed that he instinctively recoiled from them with childlike intuition whenever they did so. The 'parting shot' that they left with me as they exited the premises on one of those occasions filled me with the most intense fear and dread. "Nice kid that," they said. "Just at the age where people, if they have the right amount of money, would like to adopt." When they had gone, I dropped to my knees in the middle of the room and crouching in a foetal position, hugged myself. I could not stop sobbing. Wesley was out in the yard playing. Of course, there is no way that I would let him see me like that. Then I prayed and began to feel stronger.

When I tune in to the channel on our TV that carries Christian programmes, I sometimes hear preachers talking about faith as if there was something innately wrong with anyone who was not 'living in total victory and spiritual assurance'. That certainly does not parallel with my reality. I experience a sense of faith when I am in the middle of the most intense personal struggle. Surely courage is only present, or even needed, in the context of threat or fear. Many times I consider myself spiritually weak but perhaps one day, when I look back on this, I might discover that I have been braver than I thought I had been. I don't know.

Anyway, I think I need to write something positive now. So let me think where to start. An example would be when the other day, I was working the streets of Tallinn - something that was unusual, as the vast majority of the time my duties take me outside the city centre itself. It was then that I saw it - 'Raekoja Plats' the very street name that I had dreamt about over two years ago. I recognised both the cafe and the church. The man of my own age that I had seen in the dream was not there of course and his features have never become clearer in my imagination. I went into the church and I sensed in the back of my mind that I had once climbed the steps to its tower. I went to the cafe as well but it evoked no particular memories for me at all.

I am almost afraid to write the next thing down. I would not consider recording it for a moment had I not discovered the perfect place to hide my journal, which at the moment only consist of a couple sheets of paper - Olga has the rest.

The other day I had trouble sleeping and had been tossing and turning all night. In the morning the metal frame of my bed seemed to be a bit wonky. I looked to see if there was any way I could adjust its stability and discovered that the leg was in fact hollow and had a rubber stud at the end to stop it marking the tiled floor. I have decided to hide this inside there, as I am confident that no one will ever find it.

So here goes. I was traveling through Tallinn - not in the very centre as it's all pedestrianised, given it is an historically protected area. I was on an arterial road. I had just boarded a bus when I heard someone call out. I initially paid no attention but eventually turned to examine the direction from which the sound was coming. A man, outside the vehicle, seemed to be calling out the name of a woman, so I turned round to see who in the bus he might be addressing but no one on board seemed to connect with him. I then turned back and to my great surprise, it was clear that he was looking directly at me. I had just taken my seat by the window and the bus was already starting to slowly move away. To my absolute astonishment he then proceeded to run alongside the bus as he tapped onto my window, in an attempt to catch my attention. Within moments the bus had left him far behind. But not before I had, in an instant, recalled who he was, though I could not recollect his name. In my mind I saw his wife's face too. Instinctively, I connected them with an apartment that I had once rented and I was certain that its location was right there in Tallinn. That couple had been my landlords! He had addressed me as Celia and I suddenly realised that that must be my real name. I was not Tania at all and for all I knew, my surname was also probably not Edwards either. And if that was my name, was my husband who had died, the father of my boy, really called Tom? If they had invented a name for me then it is more than likely that they had invented a name for him - perhaps to throw me off the scent if ever my memory began to return. And that seems to be what is happening now.

I have had no medical attention at all since the birth of my son and had virtually been left to my own devices. Had I had access to a doctor, I would have had him or her tell me if, should my memory ever return, would it return in dribs and drabs or would it come tumbling back all at once?

At least now I was aware where at least some of the pieces of the jigsaw were beginning to fit. As in an actual puzzle, there are always clusters that seemed to effortlessly lock together and others that appear to have no correlation at all with the rest. As I noted before in my journal a long time ago, I wished I had a 'picture on the box' from which to reference - but of course, I haven't. What is also abundantly clear is how many of the pieces are still missing.

There is also a further conundrum that I have been trying to deal with. I had been lying in my bed after a frustrating hour convincing Wesley to settle down and was relishing the pleasure of hearing his gentle breathing across the room in confirmation of the fact that he had at last fallen to sleep. For some reason, I started thinking about the TV moment that took place a couple of years ago when I had been in the kitchen when there was a Jack Ryan film playing in the other room. I remembered how strange it was that, when someone was calling Jack, I found myself instinctively leaving what I was doing and making my way in a reflex reaction towards the other room. I remembered at the time thinking that it was odd but now an idea had come to me. If my name is Celia and not Tania could my husband's name not be Tom, as I had been told, but actually Jack?

I have convinced myself that these two pieces of the puzzle do actually fit. What I am not sure about is whether I should mention this to Olga. She is my best friend in the world, in fact my only friend, but could I trust her? In any other context the answer would be a no-brainer but this was different. If I had to make a choice between loosing my son and passing on information that might have him taken away from me, I know what I would do. If she were to make a similar choice between me and the safety of her family, who would win? I did not believe, despite all that we meant to one another, that it would be me. And so I decided to keep the matter to myself. Anyway, what if I told her and she, in all innocence, inadvertently used my real name in the presence of others. How catastrophic would that be?

Anyway, here I am with a broken ankle. I had been trailing someone who the organisation had regularly used as a drug courier. My handlers had suspected him of syphoning off some of the drugs, or some of the cash, for himself. There was not a lot of money involved but 'face' is a big thing to these people and not only did they want to secure evidence against him, I suspect they also intended to make an example of him too.

I have become pretty proficient at what I do but at some point I must have made an error of judgment, given that while under surveillance, he turned and looked directly at me. As our eyes locked I knew in an instant that he knew what was going on. Now it was I that was the prey rather than the hunter. He moved from his position about fifty metres away and instantly accelerated towards me. I quickly moved from a saunter to a walk and then to a run. Seeing the entrance to an underground station, I clambered down the steps towards the platform. I knew what I had to do and had completed the same manoeuvre a number of times in the past whilst being trained. It was all about timing, as these things so often are.

The doors of the tube were open as the passengers were taking the opportunity to alight. The man was closing in on me. I jumped aboard and waited just seconds as he boarded a compartment further down the platform. In the split second before the electric doors closed, I jumped from the train back on to the platform. He saw what I had done and moved light lightening towards the exit but he was too late. The doors had shut automatically and the train was now moving. I saw him look with fury in the direction of where he assumed I would be but I was out of sight. I was out of sight because, in my haste to vacate the train, I had not looked where I was landing. I had not seen the suitcase standing next to a waiting passenger. My shin had glanced off its edge causing me to land awkwardly. The pain and the odd angle my ankle had adopted, left me in no doubt I had seriously damaged something.

I had been told in training that if ever I was hurt, the last thing that I should do was to call for assistance. They did not want police or ambulance crews asking questions. The rule was that I was to phone a number that they had put on my speed dial. I edged towards a bench. The pain was excruciating. Several people offered to call for assistance but I politely, but firmly, declined their kindness, arguing that I had 'Just stumbled but would be alright in minute if only I could sit down'. I called the number and waited. It did not take long for someone to arrive.

So I am stuck at home. I thought I would revert to a stack of administrative tasks - translation work, reports and spreadsheets and although there has been some of that, they are now trying to add a new string to my bow - photography.

They have given me the latest Canon digital SLR that has only recently been released the EOS 7D. They have supplied it, not with the standard lens but with an adjustable telephoto. I have been commissioned to get to grips with the manual and to use their words, 'Learn to use it like a Pro.'. I have to admit that it is not the worst task that I have been given and apart from that, it's a huge bonus being able to spend more time with my son.

Yesterday Angelika turned up with her two children. Someone had forgotten to tell her that I was incapacitated. She seemed genuinely concerned when she saw the plaster cast on my ankle. She was about to leave when I suggested she might stay for a coffee. No sooner had she arrived than the three children started bouncing off one another in anticipation of a couple of hours together. She looked back at them and then at me and clearly made the decision that she did not want to be the means of curtailing their fun - and anyway, what was she going to do with the extra time she now had on her hands?

She was happy to take care of making the coffee and we sat opposite one another in my small room as the children played out in the yard. It was lovely to listen to their laughter. I remember it as the sound of total innocence in a context oppressed by so much evil. I glanced across at Angelika and it appeared that she was perhaps thinking the same thing. She was quiet for a few seconds as her eyes scanned my face like a bar-code reader over an item of grocery. It seemed that she was trying to reach a decision and was unsure of what route to take. And then her face relaxed, as it seemed her mind had landed at one side of the fence it had been perched upon.

She began to speak and a feint smile lit up her features - so unlike the false smiles of my handlers. When it reached her eyes, I noticed for the first time how pretty she was.

As we chatted she told me her story. After an hour or so it became clear that she had previously known as little about me as I had known about her. For my part I related only the bare bones of my situation - that I had suffered memory loss and that I was held here against my will. I told her a little of what they required of me - focusing more on the administrative roles than the surveillance. She said that it was fortunate that this was all that they expected me to do. We both knew what she meant and though it seems strange me writing these words now, the thought of what she was suggesting had never really occurred to me before. I had never been approached inappropriately. Anyone with an interest in that direction would possibly have been reigned in by them. Those who were controlling me would not want the additional complications that such a scenario may incur.

It turned out that she had been brought up in the poorest of families and had married early - more to escape life at home than for any romantic reasons - although the man she had met had been good to her and treated her well. Before long they were very much in love and then the two children had been born - first her daughter and then her small son. Work that paid anything but the barest minimum was hard to come by and like so many people in their situation, they became attracted by the easy money that living outside the law offered them. Her husband had not been a violent man she told me. As she spoke she twirled a gold crucifix that hung around her neck. It seemed to give her some tactile comfort as the tips of her fingers ran over it.

The organisation seemed to have used her husband more as a messenger than anything else. She spoke of an attack at a club used by the gangs. Shots had been fired and during the confusion, her husband had been killed. He had just been in the wrong place at the wrong time. The organisation had shown no compassion or taken any responsibility, either for her or her family. When she had asked them how she was going to live, they had simply shrugged their shoulders saying that it was not their problem and such things 'go with the territory'. However, as time went by they agreed to put bits and pieces her way - like the job she was doing now. It was little more than babysitting. In fact that is exactly what it was. However, from their perspective it kept her 'in the fold' as it were and put some food on the table. It appeared that she had to share her small apartment with another family.

As I listened to her, I came to the conclusion that my situation was better than hers in a number of respects. At least I had some privacy. Confinement worked two ways and in comparison to her, there was almost a measure of safety in it.

By the time that she expressed the need to leave, and the children had rallied reluctantly to her side, I realised that I had really warmed to her. Obviously our connection was not on the same level as that which I enjoyed with Olga, but I felt that we had at least come to appreciate one another's situation and that there was empathy as well as sympathy between us.

As I prayed that night I included Angelika in my petitions. What kind of future did she and the children have to look forward to I wondered? Our situations paralleled to some degree but in other areas they did not. For example, she had no education or skills and I had had a university background. I concluded that must have been the case or I could not have been working at the level that I had otherwise. If ever this nightmare ended, at least I had options. Naturally speaking I could see few for her.

It seemed odd that though I still could not remember many things at all from my past, I was able to somehow 'feel things' about the period before I ended up here. When I had walked into that cafe in Tallinn I did not recognise anything but I definitely did 'feel' something. I certainly was aware that the church had some special significance for me though, whatever it was, I had been unable bring it to the surface. So much was still submerged.

The one thing that was a 'common denominator' between us was that we were both widows. And then another thought surfaced. Could I really be sure even about that? If I had been lied to about my identity and my husband's identity, could I not also have been lied to about his death? Was it even remotely possible that he was still alive? Furthermore, if that was the case, wherever he was right now, he must be assuming that I was dead. The idea both thrilled me and filled me with dread. Firstly, none of this may be true and I could be wasting my future by living in false hope. Secondly, if it was true, and if he believed me to be dead, could he have met and married someone else? As my mind began to work through those permutations, the next realisation that came to me, was that if he was alive he certainly would have no idea at all that he now had a son.

Christmas had come and Christmas had gone. Olga had of course been with her parents and Angelika with her children. I had thought of asking Angelika and her family to spend either Christmas Day or Boxing Day with us. Wesley would have loved that and I had no doubt that, had the opportunity be offered them, they would have come. However, I had to think of the signal that it would send to our handlers. At the moment they see Angelika as a pawn that they are controlling. They probably ask her questions about me, though on a different level to the way they would interrogate Olga. Olga is supposed to bond with me but Angelika is not. She is there not only to watch over Wesley while I am working but to ensure that I am not allowed off the premises with him. If they thought for a moment that a friendship was evolving between the two of us, it would be sure to ring alarm bells in their minds. There are lines that cannot be crossed for her sake as well as mine.

She came on New Year's Eve. I had been detailed to an assignment and had got in later than usual. However, when I returned home, Angelika did not seem in the least put out, though her children appeared fretful and tearful. It had been a long day for them and they were tired. I did not want to detain her with small talk, assuming that she also would be anxious to get home. I asked if she was to be part of any celebration later that night and she said not, adding that all she wanted to do was to get the children home, bathed and to bed, rather than seeing in the New Year. She would be retiring for the night, she told me, at the first opportunity.

Shepherding the children towards the door, she stopped, turned round and came towards me. She fell into my arms and to my surprise, began to weep uncontrollably.

"I can't face another year like this," she said through her sobs. She told me that the pressure was getting too much for her. I held her for a few minutes in an effort to comfort her and when she eventually pulled away and moved back towards the door, startled me with the words, "Both of us need to free ourselves from this nightmare Tania. I know it cannot be done without enormous risk and I also know that I do not have the intelligence to even begin to imagine how such a thing could come about. But I know for sure that you could come up with something. I feel I have already said too much but I totally trust you. Please give it some thought… please Tania. Please get us all out of this!" And with that she was gone.

Celia 2010 February

I haven't seen Olga for weeks, and then out of the blue, I hear that she will be coming tomorrow. In the meantime, my relationship with Angelika has become somewhat odd. Nothing wrong, nothing wrong between us at all. It's just that something is strange. After the emotional parting on New Year's Eve, I thought she might open up a bit more or develop further what she had expressed about the need to extricate herself from her dilemma. Yet she has said nothing more - not raised a thing. She just interacts with me as if everything is 'business as usual'. I haven't felt it appropriate to bring this up from my end. After all, it was she who initiated the move in the first place. I imagine she has regretted making herself vulnerable and has worried that she had confided in me to the degree that she had. She obviously knows that part of my role is to spy on those working for the organisation and it could well be that she is anxious that I might relate to the people controlling me what I had discovered about her. I can only hope that, as some time has now past and there have been no repercussions on her, that she will soon feel a little easier about her situation.

When Olga came I told her what had happened and I asked her what connection or relationship there was between her and Angelika. She told me, that apart from knowing that she existed and the role that she played as far as Wesley and I were concerned, she had very little connection at all. However, she did find it interesting and said that she might be an asset at the point that we decided to make a move. Although, she pointed out that there could also be complications. And when she explained them to me, I had to say that I tended to agree with her. This new development was a double-edged sword. Any plan of action, if executed, would mean that the three of us, and the children, would have to be taken into consideration. With so many extra variables in the equation, a false step in any direction could prove disastrous for all of us.

It was at this meeting that Olga told me that she would be travelling to the UK in a few days. There were some people she said that she had been asked to shadow. Something to do with a past operation that had gone wrong. It seemed to be something to do with a damage limitation exercise of some sort as far as I could make out. She mentioned Gloucestershire and I instinctively knew that was in the Cotswolds. Perhaps it was something I had picked up from the TV, or on the other hand, part of the increasing database of awareness that I had filed away in the recesses of my pre-traumatised mind.

Something else also happened while she was with me. She had brought a briefcase with her. She often did. I believe she did paperwork whenever she travelled by train. She had asked if she could use my small bathroom to take a shower and I had said that of course she could. I could hear the water running but over that sound I heard a mobile ringing. I instinctively looked towards mine but it then became clear it was coming from her briefcase. I went to the bathroom door to let her know her phone was ringing - in case the call had been urgent. Wesley was in the room with me. Olga called through the door that she would not come out, but would I open the case and pass the handset to her, as she needed to take it. I flicked the two latches on the case, retrieved the phone and scurried across the room to the bathroom in the hope I got there before whoever it was rang off. She switched off the shower, opened the door, took the phone and proceeded to answer the call.

Coming back into the room I saw that an inquisitive Wesley was playing with the still opened briefcase. I told him that he should not do that and to leave it alone. I was closing the lid when I saw an A4 sized manilla file. Wesley had jostled the papers inside it and I went to place them back in the folder. It was then that I saw the top sheet. It had the laminated photo of a man fixed by a paperclip to the top right-hand edge. The name underneath was 'Damian Clarke'. I knew that I had seen that face somewhere before but had not got a clue where. I head the click of the bathroom door. I patted the papers in place within the file and closed the lid.

Although Olga and I trusted one another implicitly, I did not want her to think I was rummaging through her file, for the very same reason I did not want Angelika to think that I was spying on her. What a complicated web of subterfuge I had been drawn into - a world where even friends were forced to be suspicious of even those closest to them. The click of the case coincided with Olga's re-emergence back into the room, enveloped in a large towel. Her left arm held it in place as her right hand held the mobile that she was speaking into.

When I went to bed that night, I had the strangest of dreams. I read somewhere that dreaming is used as a devise for the brain to unscramble the complex incongruities of our waking hours. I dream a lot these days but when I emerge from sleep, any memories that I retain, leave me without the slightest semblance of anything clear or coherent. Usually the images are bizarre and meaningless. My dream on that occasion was unusually simple, by virtue of the fact that it did not seem in any way surreal. On the contrary, it was a simple scenario. I was attending a funeral and once it was over, I found myself travelling on a plane. One of the people that was accompanying me was the very man whose photo I had seen on the file. The other was his wife, who was introduced to me as someone called Sue. The only thing that did not ring true, was that she spoke about the man whose funeral we had attended and who everyone referred to as 'Wesley'.

Olga 2010 March

Olga climbed the concrete stairwell to the landing that gave access to her parent's apartment. She had so often wanted them to move from this graffiti-covered area with its rancid smells and awful shabbiness. She had also lost count of the times she had offered them the money and the times she had been lovingly rebuffed. "He is too ill to move," her mother had always argued. "It's not just the physical side of things. It's not that we have got much furniture after all. It's the emotional stress, Olga. It's leaving people around here that we have known for all our lives. All our friends are here you see."

She tapped the door and was shocked to see the tired and drawn woman who appeared in front of her. It was as if her mother had somehow shrunk in size since she had last visited her. Her eyes were sunken and dark rimmed. When the older woman recognised her daughter, the same eyes moistened and glistened in recognition.

"Olga, dear. It's so wonderful to see you. Your father will be so delighted that you have come."

Her mother took her hand and led her towards a bedroom door, in the same way she would have done when Olga was a child and as if she could not have found her own way along the short passage without her help. Olga knew what was happening of course. She was being 'mothered'. It was her way of saying, "You're a grown and sophisticated lady, but you are still my little girl."

If she thought that her mother had declined in health since she had seen her last, that was nothing in comparison to the form she saw laying on the bed in front of her. Her father, with obvious difficulty, slowly turned his head as his daughter entered the room. His face was almost skeletal and she could see by the outline that the sheets made as they covered his frail form, that his body reflected the same demise.

"It's so lovely to see you Olga," he said, as his eyes motioned her to the simple wooden chair in the corner of the room.

Olga drew it closer to the bed, without for a second removing her gaze from her father's face, and sat down. She instinctively knew that he wanted to say something that was of great importance to him and that it was a struggle for him, even to speak.

"You know I have not got long, don't you love?"

"Oh Dad…."

"No, let him speak," his mother interrupted. "He has something to say to you and you should listen. We have had a long talk and knew that you would be coming as soon as you could. So let him go on. What he has to say will be difficult for you to hear in more ways than one."

"You know that I have nothing to leave you."

"Dad, please…."

"Olga, what did I just say? Don't interrupt him dear," her mother enjoined as she came across to where she was sitting and laid her hand gently on her shoulder, as if in support for what was coming next.

Olga felt a chill going down her spine.

"You know I have nothing to leave you," her father went on. "And your mother and I know that I could not have had the medication and financial support that I have received if it was not for you."

"But Dad…."

Olga's mother gently squeezed her shoulder and Olga let her father proceed.

"You have always left us with the impression that the career you have, has made it all possible. I could never understand what you do - too complicated for someone like me - but you need to know that I am aware of where it really comes from."

"My friend, who inadvertently related to me the reason why I had an uninterrupted supply of drugs, was the same person who conveyed the last batch of medication. He said that he had overheard two things very recently and he felt that I needed to be told - I should say warned - in advance. The first thing that he overheard, was the doctor telling one of the members of the organisation that I was about to die and that this would be the last delivery. The second thing that he overheard, and you will now know why you must not attend the funeral, is that as they will have no further control over you and as you know so much about their activities, they intend to kill you."

Olga's hand rose to her mouth. She could see how tired her father was and how much the ordeal of relating this was taking out of him but he continued to speak.

"They know that you have a passport and documents and can get to any place you want to quickly, so they plan to attack you immediately after the funeral. They are of course convinced that you will be there. But Olga you must not be!"

"But what about my mother?"

"Your mother will be alright. She is not a threat to them. She knows nothing. However, when they see that you are not at the funeral they may attempt to get to you through her. We have already sorted that out between us."

Olga was speechless. She had lived in a world of planning, subterfuge and deceit for years, and here were her parents - ordinary and uncomplicated people - arranging for matters beyond her father's decease and organising a plan of escape from a criminal gang! It was beyond belief.

"We have distant family friends. I don't even think that you have met them. They live a long way from here and no one would be able to trace us to them. We took a huge risk. We took them into our confidence. We are glad that we did. The moment the funeral service is over your mother is to slip out of the side door of the church. They will be waiting in their car, it's more of a van really, which is good as the few possessions that have a significance to her will already be stored inside. They will take her directly from the church to their home. I must sleep now Olga dear, and you must go. Spend some time with your mother of course but let me get some rest. There is just one thing more I want to ask of you."

"Anything, father, anything," Olga said, with tears welling up in her eyes and making their way to her cheeks.

"I want you to let me pray with you. I know that sounds strange my dear and for many reasons. I have hardly been a spiritual influence over your life, though I must say, even with all my limitations, I have sought to be a good father. I also know that matters of faith perhaps do not have the same level as importance for you as it does with your mother and me."

"Father, of course you can pray for me. Of course you can. I want you to."

Now the tears were flowing freely and Olga slid from her chair to her knees and nestled her head against her father's shoulder. He slowly edged his arm around her, cradling her as she lay there, as he had done all those years ago when she was just a little girl. He prayed God's blessing over her and when he finished, she stayed a few moments longer in that position before rising to her feet, kissing his forehead and slowly leaving the room.

She sat with her mother and talked for several hours. Olga expressed how difficult it would be not to attend her father's funeral but realised that her mother would never be at peace until she had given her assurances. Before she left she looked into her parent's bedroom and saw her father was asleep. She did not feel that she could wake him, even though she so much wanted to say goodbye. Even though she knew that this may well be the last time that she would see him alive.

Mother and daughter hugged one another and Olga made her way out to the landing. Walking, for the final time down the stone steps, she made her way back onto the street.

Two days later Olga was on a flight to Birmingham in order to track a man called Jack Troughton. When that phase of surveillance was concluded, within hours of arriving back in Estonia, she would feel as if all the pieces of her life had been thrown up into the air and were on a downward trajectory searching for a place to fall. The shape that the pattern would take was very much open to question.

Jack 2010 April

When Jack had returned from London, the first person that he contacted to update on the situation was Damian. He had assured him that it was obviously OK for him to share whatever he wanted with Sue. The problem was, how fair was it that his friends knew and his mother was still in the dark about the fact that there was a possibility, however remote, that Celia was still alive? Nevertheless, he had concluded that the time was not yet right to put that burden on her. There was little point in doing so until there was at least some more concrete evidence. And then there was Simon in Edinburgh. He would have to know.

Jack was due to spend some time with his mother up in Scotland, so it made sense to talk to Simon face to face when he visited the Edinburgh, rather than trying to explain everything over the phone. Simon Bellenger had been with the charity from its earliest days. He had never met Celia personally, as the accident in which she had been involved had taken place before he had even met Jack. But all the refuge homes around the country for women who had been trafficked had been named 'Celia Centres' in honour of her. There was no way that he could be kept out of the loop.

Jack picked up his iPhone and hit the speed dial for his friend's number.

"It seems ages since I last heard from you stranger," Simon said, as he recognised the caller ID and answered the call. "Where are you ringing from? Are you in Manchester or on the road?"

"I'm phoning from the car. I am on the M74 en route to Mum's place and I wondered if we could meet up in the next day or so. I've got some news that you will not believe and I don't want to talk about it on the phone. Is that a possibility? How are you fixed?"

"Of course it's a possibility. Do you want to drive over to Livingston or will you be dropping in to the office?"

"Neither," said Jack, after pausing momentarily to consider the options. "I need to do some shopping in Edinburgh at some point and I wondered if we could meet up for lunch, say on Princess Street, would that work?"

"I could do that as early as tomorrow actually, I need to be in town myself," replied Simon.

"That's great. Then how about meeting up at the Caledonian, the hotel just below the castle?"

"That's good for me but it's a bit pricey Jack."

"It's on me Simon. We need somewhere where we can talk - and that's a comfortable option where we don't feel that we need to move on should we run over time. You know how it is in some places."

"This must be some news Jack if you are going to all this trouble. Can't you give me a clue?"

"I'm sorry, I really can't. Not on the phone. Is it OK if I book a table for 12:30? Would that fit in with your schedule?"

"12:30 is fine," responded Simon. "And by the way, I've got some pretty exciting news myself that I want to tell you. I think it might even trump anything that you have got to tell me."

"I hardly think so Simon," responded Jack confidently. "I hardly think so!"

The commissionaire nodded towards Jack, as at 12:20 on the following day, he entered the grand entrance of the Caledonian. He had never stayed there as his mother's place was only an hour away. But on special occasions, if he had an important appointment, there were few places better in the beautiful city of Edinburgh, that many referred to as the 'Athens of the North'. The commissionaire always greeted him as if he was one of the hotel's most valued guests. But Jack concluded that he probably had the knack of doing that with almost everybody he recognised.

Simon was already in the lobby when Jack arrived and on seeing his friend enter, rose to greet him, as they made their way off in the direction of the grandly named restaurant, 'Pompadour by Galvin'.

"So who is going to share their news first?" asked Simon, once they had taken their table, declined the wine list and ordered their first course.

"I think it should be you," suggested Jack. "Let's hear it. I bet it's some new scheme you have for the Centre. Or is it perhaps something grander - such as a suggestion you have for the charity as a whole?"

"I'm getting married Jack!"

"You are what?" said Jack in total surprise.

"You heard me. I'm getting married to the most wonderful woman in the world. Of course, I know that everyone says that don't they when they announce an engagement but nevertheless that's how I feel."

"I never even knew you were seeing anyone," said Jack incredulously. "I am supposed to be one of your closest friends. Why would you have kept something like that quiet? If this woman is so important to you - why the big secret? Obviously I don't have any right to know - I am not suggesting that – it's just that it seems so odd."

Simon made no attempt to interrupt or argue. He thought it best to just let Jack continue. Naturally he knew how he must feel and when it seemed that his friend had said everything that he felt he needed to say, then he would time the bombshell appropriately.

"Apart from anything else," Jack went on, "when Damian and Sue met you on the New York cruise that they and my mother were on, you had just come out of a Gay relationship. By the time I was introduced to you and invited you to join the team, and right up until the present time, I have never known you to date anyone. I know becoming a Christian had a massive impact on you, as it did on me, but I just assumed that you had chosen a celibate lifestyle. Obviously I am absolutely over the moon, and so will all our friends be when they hear."

Jack paused for a moment and then considered his words before he continued.

"By the way, I should ask, where am I in the pecking order of this revelation. Do Damian and Sue know yet? My mother and my aunt?"

"You are the first to know Jack, I promise you. Nobody knows about it from the lady concerned either. We have both decided to keep it a secret until now."

"But why would you need to do that?" asked Jack. "Please don't get me wrong. I am not suggesting that you should have mentioned it to me first and certainly not that you should ask for my approval or anything like that, but given our friendship, I at least thought…"

There was a silence - a hiatus in which Simon did not speak but just looked across the table at his friend. It seemed like an age until the next three words were uttered.

"It's Elena, Jack."

It's something of cliche to think at such a moment that 'it seemed that the air had been sucked out of the room'. But that was exactly how Jack felt.

"Your first course sir."

They had not noticed the two waiters as they laid plates before the diners, making a slight bow and moving off to leave them to their meal.

Jack was the first to speak.

"Elena, we are talking about the same Elena?"

"How many Elenas do we know Jack? It's the Elena that was a passenger in the other vehicle when Celia was killed. It's the Elena that was the only survivor from the shipping container of trafficked women found in Estonia. It's the Elena who lost the child she was carrying as a result of the accident. It's the Elena that I first met when she visited the Celia Centre where I was speaking about the work of our charity. And I also know Jack that it is the Elena who was the only woman you ever dated since Celia was killed."

"I didn't 'date' her Simon," Jack interrupted. "I took her out for a couple of meals but both of us knew that there was no future for our relationship other than friendship. She was not ready for anything more and frankly neither was I. We knew, of course, that we would always be friends. It was absolutely clear to us both that our relationship would always be platonic and nothing more."

Jack was unsure how to continue. There were things that he must say - had to say, but how could he do it without sounding patronising, and even worse, condescending.

Simon, always so sensitive and intuitive, caught the mood and knew precisely what was going through his friend's mind, so interrupted in order to make things easier.

"How can someone with my background, and someone with her history, ever hope to make a successful marriage? That's what you are really thinking isn't it?"

"She's been through hell and back," said Jack

"I know she has," responded Simon. "She's told me everything. I know she told you a lot but she has shared things with me that even you may not be aware of."

"And you think it could really work?" enquired Jack.

"Of course I do," I would not have dreamt of asking her to marry me if I was not sure. Naturally, there will be challenges but there are in all relationships aren't there? Her baptismal text…"

"Her baptismal text?" interjected Jack. "You mean she has been baptised, has become a Christian? I knew she was close to it when I talked with her, but she had so many questions and never seemed ready to, you know, 'cross the line'. I suppose it was because of all she had suffered. I understood and never felt it was right to push things like that with her. Heaven only knows what she has had to endure. She told me it was not as bad as what some of the other girls had gone through, but nevertheless."

"Well she has been baptised and is as every bit as committed to her faith as I am," said Simon. "There were five people baptised that Sunday and each one was given a scripture that the minister felt was the most appropriate for each of them. Elena's was 2 Corinthians 5:17."

I know it well," said Jack. It is an amazing verse for her - for all of us really - but so appropriate for Elena - 'If anyone is in Christ, the new creation has come. The old has gone, the new is here'. Wonderful!"

"That verse is special to us both," said Simon. "And we want to make that the basis of our new life together."

"Well, I am totally thrilled for you both and all our friends will be too when you tell them. I obviously won't say anything until you make the announcement public. When do you think that will be?"

"I think that now you know - we both wanted you to be the first - we can go public. We don't want it to be a secret any more. We have not set a date yet but when we do, I would be honoured if you would be my Best Man."

"The honour will be entirely mine, I assure you. You can be certain of that," assured Jack.

The first course had been finished before Simon said, "Well Jack, what about your news? That's the reason why we arranged to meet here in the first place wasn't it? You did say that your news would trump mine, but I think we both agree, that is now going to be something of a stretch."

They asked that their coffees be served in the lounge and it was only when they were both seated and settled that Jack began.

"You know when you first told me about Elena earlier, you said that she was a passenger in the vehicle that collided with Celia's car, when Celia died?" said Jack.

"Yes I do," answered Simon.

"Well my friend," responded Jack, "it seems that there is a possibility that Celia may well have survived and may still be very much alive."

Celia 2010 April

As I am writing my journal today, it occurs to me, that before I pass any more of the pages on to Olga, that I check there is nothing in them that gives too many references about my relationship with her. I can't be sure that she reads what I give her but I assume that she does. Probably I would do so if it were the other way around. I have already deleted the sections about my memory returning. If she has been reading them and sees that, then she probably would just assume that the crossings-out were things that I had decided that I did not want included as they were irrelevant.

Perhaps the journaling has to come to an end anyway and has served its purpose.

So what is it then that I have been able to recall? Well, there is the fact that I recognise several areas of Tallinn and sometimes even know, before I turn a corner, the name of the road I am about to enter - and I am almost always right. The medieval old town has become especially familiar and I am totally at home among the tall towers with their ochre-coloured pointed slate roofs. The church with the steps to its own tower is particularly poignant I feel, as is the café, in which I am sure that I spent time with my husband. The person I now am convinced is called Jack.

The more I think about the man who tried to attract my attention as the bus was drawing away, the more I am sure that he was the person from whom I once rented an apartment. I can also see his wife clearly in my mind's eye and the flat itself I can visualise as if I was in it only yesterday.

Damian Clarke, whose name and picture I saw on Olga's file, I am sure I know too - and I am similarly sure his wife's name is Sue. It somehow feels that, though I sense they had no long-term connection with me, I do believe that they must have been friends - perhaps even close friends of Jack and myself.

What really has been puzzling me of late, is the dream about me sitting next to Damian on a plane coming back from the funeral of someone with the name of Wesley of all people. That really is very odd. Why would I give my baby that name anyway? Was it because I liked the sound of it or was it that in my 'Christian past' I had an affection for the name of John or Charles Wesley the founders of Methodism? I can't think that would be the case, surely not. Or was it I wonder, that deep in my subconscious there was a recollection of someone in either my family or Jack's that had the same name? Perhaps that is it - or maybe I am barking up the wrong tree. One thing I am entirely convinced of however, is that I was a Christian long before my accident. My faith has become increasingly important to me and without doubt, has been my primary anchor during these horrendous years.

Angelika has been far more natural with me of late. I am convinced that her earlier reticence was due to her concern that she had opened up to me too much and was worried that I might betray her confidence. As time has passed, and she has seen that I have not done that, she seems to have relaxed a great deal.

The only thing that ties her to these dreadful people is her dependence on them for an income; and the reason that they continue to allocate her small sums is that, if she were to leave their orbit of influence, they would be worried about how much she knows. She would have no understanding of the core of the criminal enterprise, as I do via the spreadsheets, but will certainly have picked up a lot about their day to day operations.

The thing is she has nowhere to run and no money with which to escape - pretty much like me really. If they tire of her, they are unlikely to draw her into the trafficking area of their business. They are more likely just to dispose of her and if that were the case, I absolutely dread to think what would happen to the children. How she sleeps at night I do not know.

Olga sent me a note to say that she will be dropping in on me but is not sure when - that's really strange because so much of her schedule is planned in advance by her handlers.

Olga and Celia 2010 April

Olga rang the bell at Celia's apartment at 9 p.m. She never normally visited this late in the evening but this was going to be anything but a normal call. She could feel her heart pounding in her chest as she waited for the door to be opened. Eventually it did, though only slightly, as it was held by a safety chain. When Celia recognised it was Olga she momentarily closed the door to release the chain and then invited her friend inside.

"I am really sorry to drop in on you so late Tania, and totally unannounced too. Something really important has happened that I needed to make you aware of as soon as I possibly could," said Olga in a breathy whisper, as she considered that it was likely that Wesley had been put to bed and was anxious not to wake him.

"Slow down," said Celia reassuringly. "Look, come through and settle down and I will put the kettle on – tea or would you prefer coffee?"

"No, tea will be fine for me, I rarely take coffee as late as this or I would never get to sleep. Frankly, Tania, when you hear what I have got to say, I doubt that either of us will be sleeping very much tonight anyway."

The apartment was so small that Celia could easily hear what Olga was saying from the kitchen area but waited until the tea was ready before joining her friend in the main room.

"I have to say, this sounds ominous," said Celia.

"My father has died," Olga blurted out - coming straight to the point.

"Oh I am so sorry to hear that," responded Celia sympathetically. "But…"

"No, that's not why I have come round to see you," interrupted Olga. "That news I could have given you at any other time. It's just that the implications of his death are about to impact us both."

Celia paused for a moment, trying to choose her words well and then said, "Well clearly I can see how that affects you, and obviously I am really sorry for your loss, even though I know that this is something you anticipated might happen, but impact me - in what way exactly?"

"More than you might think Tania, believe me, far more than you might think. I know you understand the back story- the fact that he, and my mother of course, was the only reason why I had anything to do with these people in the first place."

"Yes of course," said Celia. "Your father required special drugs that you could not otherwise afford, so by working for them, you ensured that he got the medication that he needed. Yes, that was always clear to me."

"But can you not see what that means?" said Olga. "Because he has now passed away, he no longer needs the drugs and they don't have the power over me that they once had."

"Yes," said Celia , "But I would have thought that that was a good thing."

"It's not a good thing at all, Tania, surely you understand that. It means that because I do not need them, and because I know so much about their operations, they see themselves as vulnerable. They obviously realised that I would never work for them out of choice, so as far as they are concerned, I am a loose cannon. I cannot be controlled as before and they have come to the conclusion that I would probably have no compunction in relating to the authorities everything that I know. I can even go further than that and assure you, that they have already put a contract out on my life."

"You're kidding me Olga?" said Celia incredulously.

"Kidding you?" continued Olga. "Why in heaven's name would I joke about a thing like that? Listen, I know for sure that it is true, because when I saw my dad for the last time, he told me that he had heard that was certainly the case . He even begged me not to attend his funeral."

"Not attend his funeral!" exclaimed Celia. "Why on earth not?"

"Because people would be waiting for me as soon as the service concluded. I even had to have my mother spirited away through a side entrance, and thank goodness, I have been able to confirm that she is in a place of safety - somewhere that even they will never find her. All the stuff you read about in novels or see on TV about tracing mobile signals and credit card usage is lost on her. She does not possess either and never has. She will be fine now, I know she will.

In one way, I took a risk even in coming here, but on balance, I felt it would be OK as they would not be aware of the level of our friendship. As far as they are concerned you are just a 'mark' that I was covering and helping to control, not one of my dearest friends."

Celia noticed the tension in Olga's body language. She was sitting rigid as she talked, her hands gripping the edges of her chair. Celia reached across and placed her hand on one of hers. As she did so, she noticed Olga's body relax as she sank back from her upright position and slumped against the back of her seat - like a balloon that had been partially deflated.

"Yes," said Celia after a moments pause. "I can fully appreciate what you are saying but how precisely does this impact me? Obviously if you have to leave, as you clearly will, and go into hiding, I am going to miss you massively but there is surely some way we can keep in touch."

"You're missing the point, Tania, you're entirely missing the point," responded Olga, with not a little exasperation in her tone and resuming her rigid upright position in the chair. "If I have to leave, then this becomes the best possible time for you and Wesley to escape too. If you don't do it now you never will, and you certainly won't be able to do it on your own. You will need help on the outside. Tania, it really is now or never."

Celia went white as the realisation of what her friend was suggesting began to sink in. She sat motionless as all the

assimilate. It never occurred to her that she would be the one reeling, shell-shocked, from the revelations that would be conveyed to her.

She had just returned from looking into the life of a man who was the husband - yes the very husband - of the person who had become the closest person to her in the world.

If Celia thought that what she had just shared had rocked her, how on earth would Celia emotionally cope with what she was now going to reveal to her? In fact, she wondered if she should say anything. However, as soon as that idea entered her mind, she dismissed it immediately. Of course she had to tell her. But how was Celia going to be able to begin to process it? She was just preparing herself to speak, when Celia spoke first.

"I am sorry if what I have told you has shocked you," said Celia. "I apologise that I did not relate everything that I had learned about myself before now. I am also sorry that I saw the stuff in your case and did not trust the strength of our friendship enough to relate what had happened."

"Stop right there, Celia," interjected Olga. "I think we both need a fresh cup of tea. I'll make it and you just sit there for a couple of minutes. Put the TV on or something. The news headlines should be on in a couple of minutes. I need the bathroom and we both need a break. You think that you have shocked me - well I think you had better brace yourself now for what you are about to hear when I get back."

Celia put on the World News channel and watched updates on an earthquake in China that had killed hundreds, a plane crash in Russia in which the wife of the Polish president had been killed and the eruption of volcanic ash in Iceland that had disrupted travel plans right across Europe.

Olga placed a tray on the coffee table that lay between them and took a deep breath as she began.

"I know that the Christian faith that you have means a lot to you. I have watched from a distance the transformation that took place in my father's life when he embraced a belief in God. I also saw how it carried him through the titanic struggles he had with his health in the

113

years before he died. You are going to need every bit of that belief Celia as you listen to what I am now about to tell you."

Now it was Celia's turn to be tense. She was sitting across from her friend with one hand up to her mouth in anticipation.

"You have to understand," Olga began, "that for my part, I have held absolutely nothing from you in the past. Also, please understand that I am not trying to make you feel bad about what you had felt right to withhold from me either. It's simply that, just until a few minutes ago, I had nothing I felt I had to share that was of any particular relevance to you. Listening to you now, however, a great many things have fallen into place. I can tell you three things right away that are going to shock you. Are you ready for this?"

Celia's hand remained over her mouth and she held it there simply nodding her assent.

"Your name is Celia, and not Tania, as you have rightly assumed and your husband's name really is Jack."

Celia's hand was down now and she gasped.

"You have just said 'is' not 'was'," exclaimed Celia. "Are you trying to tell me that my husband is alive and he was not killed as I had initially been told?"

"Absolutely," responded Olga. "He is very much alive I promise you. The surname that you share is Troughton and he was until recently, totally under the impression that you had been killed in the crash."

"Until recently you said," interrupted Celia. "What do you mean by that and how do you of all people know this to be a fact? Olga, are you absolutely sure about this? I couldn't stand it, if with the best will in the world, you had got your facts wrong and all the hope you are stirring in me will soon just evaporate because you had jumped to some wrong conclusions. How can you be so sure?"

"Well, first of all slow down Celia. I know for sure because I have seen him with my own eyes within the past few days!"

Celia's hand was now back over her mouth in disbelief as if she was trying to stifle any involuntary cry that any more revelations like this might elicit. Her eyes spontaneously darted across to the bedroom where her son was fast asleep, totally unaware that he had a Daddy, who was also unaware that he had a son.

"I know that this is a lot to take in but I can also confirm that Damian and Sue Clarke are Jack's closest friends and believe it or not, I stayed briefly in their home just a week before I saw Jack. It was only when you mentioned the Clarkes and that your name was really Celia that I was able to put 'two and two' together."

"And obviously made 'four'," said Celia - still in a state of shock.

"Because all of this has fallen into place so recently - like in the past hour or so - I am still trying hard to process it myself," Olga continued. "I have read the Clarke's file as you know but the organisations' initial interest was not primarily with them. I was conducting surveillance on them simply as a means of tracking down Jack. I will go into all that with you at some other time but for now, this is what you need to know. You were in an accident and the vehicle that collided with you was being driven by members of the criminal group that are connected with us now. Your husband watched you being taken away in an ambulance with your face covered. Everyone assumed that you were dead but of course you weren't. You had total amnesia and the organisation clearly concluded, that as so many years had elapsed and nothing had changed, that your long term memory had been irreversibly erased. They have not been aware of the flashbacks and memory recall that you were experiencing from time to time. In fact I, your closest friend, was unaware of it myself until tonight. There is something though that I can't work out however. These people are evil but they are not stupid. Why would they use me to put Jack under surveillance and use the same person to supervise you? It makes no sense. They would be taking a monumental risk that one day I might 'join up the dots'."

"But you said yourself," offered Celia, "that they had convinced themselves that my long term memory was blanked out and when you think of it, you and I are the only female operatives that they are using now. They could not ask any one *but* you to keep surveillance on me. I know they are controlling Angelika but her role is just virtually babysitting me. And by the way, I need to talk to you about her too at some point."

"I'm not following," said Olga. "What has she got to do with any future plans that we might have? If we get out she just stays behind. We can't solve everybody's problems Celia, you must surely realise that?"

"We can't just 'leave her behind' as you put it," retorted Celia.

"You have got to get yourself clear within the next few hours, I understand that. I also totally agree with you that it's 'now or never' as far as Wesley and me are concerned, though I am entirely at a loss as to how such a thing could materialise. However Olga, think this through. If we were to depart the scene, Angelika would then come immediately under the spotlight. They would not believe that she was ignorant of our intentions - well I mean my intentions really. They would interrogate her and we both know what that would entail. Even if she managed to convince them, with me gone, they would have no further use for her and she would be reduced to yet another 'loose end' that they would feel the need to 'tidy up'. No, Olga, abandoning her and just saving our own skins is just not on. She must be part of our calculation too."

"What calculation are you talking about Celia?" asked Olga in exasperation. "We don't have any calculations do we?"

"Oh I now understand what you are saying Olga," said Celia raising her voice and then immediately muting it back down to a whisper so as not to wake Wesley. "You have got an exit plan for yourself and you are going to execute it and Wesley and I would therefore just hamper your escape. We would just become ballast that would slow you down!"

As soon as the words were out of her mouth Celia regretted saying them. Everything was becoming so overwhelming and so frightening. She took a deep breath and then immediately apologised. But before she could say anything else, Olga spoke.

"Look this is massive for both of us. I am sorry if I sounded heartless Celia. We are all in a total whirl aren't we? Let's take one step at a time. I am going nowhere without you and never intended that I would. We both need one another anyway. I suggest we begin to prioritise what we need to do first, and then we will try and sort out where we can fit Angelika and her children into the equation.

The first thing I am going to do is to find a motel for a couple of days. I have somewhere in mind that no one will ever think of looking for me. I can't go back to my place where most of my stuff is, as they will have a watch on it by now. However, I managed to pack some essentials and once they realise that I am not going back and there is nothing there of interest, hopefully, at some point in the future, I can retrieve the things that I have left. I have a credit card and some cash but that is not going to last me very long, as at the moment, I am not very far off my card limit. I know that you have neither card nor cash so we will have to work with the little that I have got for now.

As I have recently traveled I have my passport and my papers in my possession. The problem is that you and Wesley don't have yours - well you do, but they are at the home of one of the two men that are controlling us. I was allocated my assignment to cover you when I was in St. Petersburg. One of them, Diak Sokolov, is still there but the other, a man called Kuznetsov, has moved over here to Tallinn. The documents are in the house where he and his wife live. I know it because I have been summoned there more than once. I know for a fact your documentation is there! I remember him sitting behind his big desk, and when he was referring to the control he had over you, he made the mistake of tapping the top of his desk, just above the left hand drawer, as he said, "That woman will not be going anywhere very far without these." The problem obviously, is how I am going to be able to retrieve them. It certainly won't be easy. They have taught me enough about alarm systems, so I can use that against them. The problem is, that though his kids are grown up and it's only him and his wife in the house, if I were to breach security, I would obviously have to be sure that they were not in the house at the time. I do have the embryo of an idea but it's a very long shot. But anyway leave that with me."

117

"But that means that you are putting yourself at very high risk on my, or our, account," said Celia, as once again her eyes flitted towards her young son's room. "It's too dangerous Olga. You could get away much easier if you just escaped on your own. You need to just go and then let me work things out for myself."

"That's not going to happen," retorted Olga. "I have already said that we need one another and that is the way that it is going to be. Look, I am going to have to leave now. It's getting very late. I am not going to be able to come back here again, you realise that don't you? Your place is going to be under surveillance very soon. When we make a move we will have to move fast. So be sure to have everything that you need already packed. As I have said, I will be able to do nothing until I secure your papers. When I have accomplished that I will write you a note. I shall get into the vicinity and then ask someone to pass the note under your door."

"And Angelika and the children?"

"Celia, I have not thought that through but I promise you that I will do my best to consider them as well - honestly! Just go with what I have suggested."

They both stood simultaneously and negotiating the coffee table, held one another in a longer-than-usual hug before Olga made her way to the door.

"Oh and by the way," Olga said turning before she left. "The name Wesley…"

"What of it?" inquired Celia.

"It's the name of Jack's father - his grandfather - something else you managed to subconsciously retain in that mind of yours! Yes and another thing, Jack is in the UK - but I assumed you realised that.

Olga 2010 April

Olga booked into the motel she had chosen, found her room, put the chain lock on the door, put down her case, kicked off her shoes and collapsed fully clothed onto the bed. What a day it had been. Never in her entire eventful life had there been a day that had come close to what she had experienced in the past twenty-four hours. She lay there for what seemed an age, just thinking and staring up to the ceiling. The plan she had in mind was beyond risky. She wanted to shower and then get to bed but there was something that she needed to do first. If she didn't, then she would never sleep tonight, however exhausted she was. She picked up her phone and found a password protected app that held all her financial details - such as they were. She checked the credit card balance, as everything she now had in mind depended on that. Having found what she was looking for, she realised that the amount 'available to spend' was even less than she had thought. But it should just be enough for what she now needed to do.

She woke late the following morning, took breakfast at a kind of diner that were often to be found next to motels such as hers, and set off towards the shopping area. She was not paranoid but she did not want to take any unnecessary risks. It would be wrong to say that she had changed her appearance to the point of disguise but nevertheless, anyone looking for her would have to look twice before they realised that it was her. The first port of call was a hardware shop, where she purchased the heaviest hammer that she was confident she would be able to wield with one hand and a crow bar. The second visit was to a pharmacy where she obtained hair colouring. By the end of the day blonde would become brunette. Under any other circumstance it would not be a choice that she would make but at least it would grow out eventually, and anyway - needs must.

When everything was done she looked at her watch and saw it was lunchtime, there was nothing more she could do for now. She did not want to return this early to a cheerless motel but on the other hand, wandering aimlessly with the chance of being spotted, when all the organisation's people in the area would be on full alert, was not an option either. She could not implement the first stage of her plan until it was dark, so her compromise was to use coffee shops in the area and stay there as long as it was reasonably possible. There was one other visit she had to make before returning to the motel and commencing the re-colouring. She had to drop in to the finest French restaurant in the city and speak to the Maitre D'.

The Kuznetsov's lived in the kind of place that was typical of criminal elements. No inherent sense of style but of accumulated wealth and a need to brandish it about. Everything about it screamed architectural bling. The new-build was part Spanish hacienda and part Greek temple - Corinthian pillars either side of the heavy oak doors clashing with the ochre coloured tiles on the roof. The ornamental fountain in the drive that led up to the house looked as though it had fallen out of the sky and settled indiscriminately on the tarmac on which it was perched. The house would never have been to her taste, even if she had the money to buy it.

The thing that would have bothered her, should she ever have the means to live in the area, was its proximity to the railway line that ran just a couple of hundred metres beyond the end of the garden to the rear. '*How on earth did they live with the rattle and the noise?*' she thought. Until she remembered an aunt of hers who also had lived in a similar situation - though in a house not nearly as opulent. When she had raised the matter with her, her aunt had said that she had quickly got used to it to the point that she didn't hear it any more. In fact, when her aunt had moved to the countryside to retire, she used to wake up at 2 a.m. every morning to the absence of the sound of the mail train that wasn't there. Tonight, hopefully the railway line was going to work to her advantage. She had done some research and trusted that her calculations would prove accurate.

She planned to break into the house in a couple of days but there was a major obstacle that needed to be overcome first. This did not relate to the security system; her training would cover that. Neither was it the motion-detecting cameras that covered the drive. It had become second nature for her to notice the security arrangements at whatever property she visited and on her previous visits here she had already seen the blind spots.

The big problem was the heavy iron double gates at the entrance to the drive. Probably the reason why the camera installers had not been over meticulous about blind-spots on the drive, was because they could never imagine anyone, however agile, scaling such a barrier. Olga had examined the gates. They were painted glossy black, the spear-like points at the top painted gold. The owners obviously considered the property to be an impregnable citadel. She didn't - at least she hoped she didn't.

At 3:30 a.m. the following morning, clad in the darkest clothes she could find, Olga approached the house. In her left hand she carried a holdall that housed the heavy hammer and the crow bar. If she had calculated correctly the train would pass by at precisely 3:37 a.m. She considered that she would have less than two minutes to do everything that needed to be done.

It was in fact 3:42 a.m. when the train hurtled by. She listened as it approached and the decibels of sound grew. Just before the noise reached its peak she swung the hammer with all her might at the locking mechanism. Her objective was not to break the gates open, as that would have been impossible. All she needed to do was to ruin the lock. The engine's ebbing sound indicated she only had seconds to go. In one final attempt to complete her objective, she positioned the crow bar with precision and brought the hammer down for the final time. It remained to be seen if she had been successful. There was no way of knowing in this light but shortly after 10:30

a.m. later that day she would find out. She glanced around, sweeping the entire street with her gaze. No lights had come on, either in the target house or in the ones nearby. Clearly the noise of the passing train had successfully muffled the sound of her activity. She made one last look to ensure that it was not just the lock area that had been affected but that the lower part of the gate had been damaged also. The marks were superficial but that did not matter.

Olga gathered her tools back into her bag and walked at a steady pace in the direction of where she was staying. As she crossed a bridge she glanced all around again. Olga heaved the holdall to the parapet and then pushed it over. The splash into the river below would have disturbed no one at that time in the morning. She also knew that, containing the weight that it did, it would be sunk deep into the mud on the river-bed only seconds later.

The taxi arrived at the front of the motel at 10 a.m. precisely - just as Olga had arranged. She indicated to the driver the name of the street that she wanted him to head for - the road in which Kuznetsov's house was situated. She needed to know that the first stage in her plan had been effective and walking past in the daylight was certainly not an option - she could easily have been spotted. She told the driver that she was looking to buy a property in the general vicinity and wanted to get a 'feel' for the neighbourhood, so would he kindly drive slowly around the area. She went on to say that when she was satisfied she had seen enough she would ask him to bring her back to the motel. It was clear from the face of the driver that he thought the request was strange but as far as he was concerned 'a fare was a fare' and as long as she paid, what she was really up to was no business of his.

As they approached the street Olga reminded the driver of his instruction. However, as he entered it he turned round to her and said, "It does not seem as if slowing down is going to be an option. It looks to me that that choice has already been made for us - there appears to be some commotion on the side of the road over there,

Miss. I think we will be down to crawl even if we don't have to stop."

Olga, who had chosen to wear a headscarf, pulled herself further back into her seat and away from sight. There were two vehicles outside Kuznetsov's place. In one of them two heavy-set workmen were heaving metal cutting equipment that they had obviously used to cut open the gates - the locks having been rendered useless. The two gates would then be taken off their hinges and loaded into the rear of the second vehicle, a small lorry. Whether the gates would be taken away to be repaired or to be disposed of because of having been rendered useless by the cutting equipment was of no consequence to Olga. The fact was that phase one of her three-point plan had been totally successful. The gates which she never could have scaled would be gone.

In order to comply with her cover story, she asked her driver to cruise slowly around a couple of adjacent streets before asking him to take her back to the motel. She had not been surprised at the absence of police cars at the location. People like Kuznetsov handled their own business. The last thing in the world he would have wanted was police snooping around his property.

As Olga lay on her bed, and looked up yet again at the drab ceiling, she felt just the smallest of smiles beginning to crease her face and there were two reasons for that. The first was that her first objective had been accomplished and she now had open access to get in at least as far as the house. The second was imagining what Celia would have said if she had asked for her prayers so that her mission of lies, subterfuge and criminal damage could be successful.

Now for stage two.

Kuznetsov had been incandescent with rage earlier that day. He had reversed his black Mercedes out of one section of the triple garage. Swinging his car round in the drive to face the exit, he noticed in his rear-view mirror the electronic garage doors closing behind him. He pressed the grey fob in his right hand to cause the electronic gates in front of him to swing open towards him. He had got the timing off to a fine art - the approach, slowing down at exactly the right distance so that he was sufficiently far from the gates for them to give him access, accelerating slowly forward and then moving out onto the street as the gates retuned to their original position. His first meeting of the day was an important one and even allowing for the morning traffic, he was well on schedule. But apparently the fob was not working. He cursed the small piece of plastic in his hands and the batteries that he assumed were the cause of the trouble. Then he controlled himself and intentionally breathed deeper and slower. The batteries were dead, so what? This was no more than a five minute delay, so no problem. He had been careful to insist that the installers fitted a manual over-ride and once he was out of the car, selected it, and was back behind the wheel, the minor crisis would be over.

But the minor crisis was not over. Neither was it a minor crisis. The manual over-ride was not functioning either. He was trapped inside his own property. When he had first looked towards the locking area he had jumped immediately to the conclusion that someone had deliberately vandalised the lock. Then, when he looked lower down the gate, he saw that the lower area was damaged as well. The issue, he decided, had clearly not been the lock but the gate itself. In fury he reversed the Mercedes back towards the house, threw the fob out of the window in anger, pulled out his phone and made two calls. It was now 7:30 a.m. and it was clear that he was not now going to be able to attend the important meeting. The first call was to explain why he would not be there. He baulked at giving the real reason, as he concluded, it would make him look a fool. The second call was to a garage but he had got no response from anyone before eight and it was a full hour later before anyone showed up.

Later that day Kuznetsov had just finished his evening meal and was trying to return to a semblance of normality, when his wife came into his study with a sealed white envelope in her hand.

"Someone must have pushed this under the door it seems," she said as she proffered it towards him. "No-one heard a sound and I've had the feed of the security camera rewound and there is nothing recorded - very odd to say the least."

Kuznetsov put down the glass of whiskey and soda he had been holding, took the envelope from her, opened it up and drew from it a single sheet of paper. His eyes widened in disbelief as he read.

"So what does it say then?" asked Kuznetsov's wife. "Why the startled look? What's going on?"

He pushed the letter back towards her and sank back with the words, "Well why don't you just read it for yourself?"

She did and mirrored a bewildered expression not dissimilar to that of her husband's.

In the early hours of this morning I was driving along your street when someone, who I assume must have been drunk, erratically sped towards me on the wrong side of the road. The driver forced me to swerve and caused me to crash into your gates. I was shaken and the offending car sped off without stopping. I had no way of contacting you during the night. This was not my fault and I am left with a damaged car. However, probably like your gates, my car is insured. As an act of good faith, and in compensation for your inconvenience, I have booked a table for you and your wife at the Maison D'Or which you will know is one of the finest restaurants in the city. The management have been given a sum of money that is sure to cover your meal and any fine wine you wish to order. Your table is booked for 7:30 p.m. tomorrow evening. The date is not transferable as I am informed this was the only available booking in the foreseeable future. You will be aware I am sure that Maison D'Or is often booked weeks in advance. Again, I am sorry for any inconvenience caused but trust that you will enjoy your meal.

"So what do you think?" Kuznetsov asked his wife.

"I don't really know. This person, whoever it is, does not want their identity revealed and I have no doubt that the restaurant have already been told not to divulge it should we enquire. In fairness, he or she did not have to do anything at all of this nature as we slept through the whole thing. At least we'll get a good meal out of it and they are absolutely right when they say that getting a table at such short notice is little short of a miracle. The Maitre D' must have been tipped well."

At 7:45 p.m. on the night in question, Olga phoned the restaurant to ensure that her guests had arrived and was assured that they were in their seats and so confirmed that the second phase of her plan had worked. All that now remained was for her to gain access to the premises, to retrieve the documents, and exit the house without being discovered. She knew that she had at least a two hour window to get the job done. The only thing to complicate matters at a time like this was the presence of a dog in the residence, but on the few occasions that she had been there in the past, she had never seen or heard one.

It was already dusk and as she had anticipated, she had no problem circumventing the security cameras. Working from the motel without a laptop at her disposal, it was clear that hacking the security system was not going to be an option. Few burglars gain access to a property via the front door unless they have a set of keys. The option of tampering with the alarm box would also be the last thing she would want to do. The most basic alarm systems would trigger in such a scenario. Many of them would also automatically relay a call to the nearest police station, or the security company, if that was attempted. She knew that this was the most unpredictable part of the whole process. She had put her faith in her ability to gain access to the rear of the property, find a vulnerable window or lock - she was adept at picking most of these devices - and so gain entry. Of course, all doors and windows would be alarmed but that would not be a problem at all, ironically, because of the training these people had given her.

On the last occasion she had been there with Kuznetsov, and they both had left the building together, he had used the keypad to arm the alarm as they vacated the house. On that occasion Olga never considered for a minute that there would be a reason to gain entrance in the future but again, it was second nature for her to notice. She had not remembered the number but she had remembered the pattern - twice to the top right, three across the middle and then the top left. If it was a standard keypad then the sequence would be 34561.

However, all this was academic, given that the wall that she had planned to scale at the side of the house, that she was confident would get her successfully to the rear of the property, had been reinforced with a modern equivalent of barbed wire - twisted bands of stainless steel. There was not a chance in the world of her getting past that.

Up to that point her biggest worry had been, once she had gained entry, was accessing the keypad by the front door in time to disarm the system. Even if she caused it to burst into life she would be able to disable it in seconds. Anyone in the neighbourhood who heard the siren start and then stop, would simply imagine it was a false alarm that had been dealt with by the occupants. Now it appeared that everything had gone up in flames just because of the one thing she had not anticipated - something as low tech and 'old school' as the barbed wire. It was bad enough that she had drained her credit card to its limit for no purpose, but far worse, that the only chance of procuring Celia and Wesley's papers had come to nothing. Without those they could not leave the country. Contacting the police for help remained out of the question, as the organisation had so many people on the payroll, across such a wide strata, that it was impossible to know who she could or could not trust.

It was dark now and all her options had seemingly evaporated. There was little point in staying around. The Kuznetsov's would be half way through their main course by now - all at her expense and all for nothing. The worst part, Olga thought, was having to tell Celia that she had failed and all that that implied. She dug her hands deep into the pockets of her anorak, not because she was cold but in some small search for comfort. As she did so she dislodged the small silver torch that she had brought for use inside the house - she could hardly have put on the lights. It had fallen to the ground. It must be on the tarmac drive somewhere, she thought, as she fumbled around for it.

Olga concluded, when she wrapped her fingers around something on the ground of a similar size, that she had found it. But as she drew

sure to search the house immediately. Carrying the packet and the papers she took out her phone and phoned the same cab company she had used earlier that day and told it where to met her.

When it arrived, she jumped in the back and gave the driver Celia's address. Today would not be a success until her friend and little Wesley were well out of the small apartment. En route she told the driver that he would need to wait outside for up to fifteen minutes - until she and a woman and a child left the apartment. Olga promised him that if he followed her instructions to the letter he would be getting the best tip he had received that week - perhaps the best tip he had received for a very long time. If the taxi driver had had a long day and was drowsily nearing the end of his shift, this certainly would serve to bring him back to life.

Olga raced up the steps and banged on the door. It was way after ten and it was likely that both mother and child would be in bed. It seemed an eternity before the door was opened and Olga was faced with a confused and bleary-eyed Celia.

"Celia, we need to leave here immediately and when I say immediately I really do mean 'now'. Did you keep your case packed with the essentials as I asked?"

"Yes, yes I did..." responded her disorientated friend. "But Wesley - he's asleep."

"Well wake the boy up and get him dressed as fast as you can," said Olga fully realising that she was sounding over-harsh but desperately trying to kick-start Celia into action.

It was probably twenty minutes before two women and a half-asleep little boy bundled themselves into the back of the taxi. The driver was offering to put their belongings into the boot but Olga told him to get back at the wheel and drive off. They would carry their bags on their laps.

"Please driver just drive off will you... right now?"

"Drive off where?" came the bemused retort. "You have not told me where I am supposed to be going."

"Just drive off to the end of this road and take a right. I'll give you the directions as we go. Just get out of the area for now and as quickly as you can."

"The driver put the cab into gear and swung right as instructed - though he nearly had a head-on collision with a large black Mercedes speeding toward him in the opposite direction.

He was just about to fill the air with a barrage of expletives when he remembered that he had two women and a child with him, so simply turned to his passengers with, "OK, where to next?"

Olga gave him the address of her motel and rummaged around at the extremities of the brown parcel that she had with her and stuffed a couple of notes in to her anorak.

"This time you will need to wait no more than five minutes," assured Olga. "My friend and her son will stay with you and all I have to do is to pick up my case."

Olga sensed as she looked across at Celia, that she was about to ask where they were going next but Olga simply put her forefinger to her lips and exited the taxi.

True to her word, she was back in the cab in the allotted time.

"So where are we off to now ladies, if you don't mind me asking and how long a pit stop are we to enjoy this time?"

"I want you to take us to the main train station but there will be one more instruction I will have for you before I pay you and you eventually see the back of us."

Olga was somewhat disconcerted to hear a huge exhaling of air. The driver was clearly not just sighing with relief but communicating that he was glad it was soon to be all over as far as he was concerned.

They pulled into the allocated taxi rank and the cab driver turned towards Olga in expectancy. He was just about to tell her the cost of the fare, to which a good tip had been promised, when Olga held up her hand to stop him.

"You have been brilliant tonight driver and we appreciate it. As I said there was one more favour I would be asking." She paused, in order to emphasise the importance of what was coming next. "Either late tonight, or some time tomorrow, it is very likely that someone

131

will approach you or your managers and ask if a woman and a boy were taken from the apartment we picked my friends up at. Please be frank and tell them that you did. The next question will be, 'Where did you take them?' To which you will answer 'the airport' not 'the station'."

Olga could see that the driver was just about to utter something in the order of, 'Well I don't know about that' when he saw the two high denomination euro notes in her hand. This was not just the best tip of the week - it was going to break all records - and his lips were immediately reconfigured to form a new response. "Well of course Miss, you can depend on me and thank you very very much."

As they stood at the curb side, Olga heard a little voice say, "Mummy did auntie Olga just ask that man to tell a lie?" Olga smiled to herself. In the past forty-eight hours she had committed criminal damage, vandalism and been guilty of both 'breaking and entry' and theft. *Yes*, she thought to herself, *I did ask him to tell a lie.*

All Celia said, as she looked towards her friend who was now illuminated by the lights of the station was, "Olga, what on earth have you done to your hair?"

Angelika 2010 April

The three of them stood at the curb side as the taxi driver accelerated into the traffic, his face beaming. Olga looked at her watch and saw that it was nearly midnight.

"So where are we going to now Olga?" enquired Celia. "Have you any idea what time it is and how exhausted Wesley must be?" *This was not the first time that Olga had appeared to 'take command' of their relationship,* Celia thought to herself - though in a way she could understand it. Olga had been her handler after all and was far more adept at navigating the city than she was - despite how much she had learned to negotiate the area herself. Nevertheless, she dreaded the thought of a train journey at this time of night - or was it morning? There was another thing: Wesley had spent almost all of his life cooped up in just a couple of rooms. Now he was being confronted by all the sights and sounds of a city at night - the traffic, the noise, the people. She had been surprised that he had not been terrified. Perhaps it was the fact that he was still only half awake, and everything was happening so fast that parts of his little brain had suspended their critical faculties at such an assault on his senses.

"We're not taking a train anywhere," said Olga, pointing to an ornate and floodlit building across the road from them.

Celia swivelled around in the direction in which her friend had pointed and drew back her head as if she was locking her gaze on a mirage in a desert.

"That's a four star hotel Olga. Are you joking? How do you imagine we are going to be able to pay for that?"

Olga drew the parcel under her arm closer to her and muttered something to the effect that it would not be a problem.

"They will be scouring the city for us and this is the last place that they will expect to look, so just follow me."

They approached the reception desk. There was, even at that time of night, a row of young men and women all in smart grey uniforms checking in the guests. Situated adjacent to the station, it was not unusual to receive customers at almost any time of day or night.

"And how can I help you?" said a pleasant woman in her late twenties as she looked across at the two women and then down at the little boy. "Do you already have a reservation?"

"No, I am afraid not." responded Olga. "We had not really anticipated having to stay but when we got off the train, we received a message to say that the person who was supposed to meet us was not able to do so - *another lie she thought to herself* - and this is our only option."

"That's absolutely fine," said the receptionist, looking down at a monitor in front of her. We have availability I see. What accommodation were you looking for exactly?"

"Ideally, one room with two single beds and a bed for the little boy. If that is not possible," Olga continued, "two single rooms next to one another would be fine."

"Yes, the first option is available," assured the woman behind the desk. "How long would you like to stay, I presume only one night if you are waiting for an onward lift - and how would you like to pay? By credit card I assume."

Olga looked across at Celia and noticed her swallowing hard. She obviously had her eyes on the 'walk-in' rates that she saw displayed on the wall.

Olga considered the probably maxed-out card and asked if cash would be possible.

"I am sorry madam we don't do cash - just credit card - it's a matter of security you see."

Olga looked crestfallen. There was a pause and then the young woman behind the desk looked as if she was remembering times when she herself had offered a card with the fear it could be rejected. Her eyes flitted between the two women and the currency in the hand of the one she was speaking to. She then glanced down once more to the tired little boy that stood alongside them and thought to herself, *These three were hardly likely to trash the room, steal the TV and raid the mini-bar.* "I'll tell you what," she said, after considering for a moment or two, "why don't you pay me in cash for one night's stay and then let me register your credit card for any little extras you might want - the bar, morning papers - things like that. In that way we have a record of your stay. That will cover the security issue and will make sure that I won't get into trouble," she added with a smile.

Olga considered this to be a perfect solution. Breakfast was already included and there would not be any extras beyond that, so the card had little chance of being rejected. When it was returned to her, together with a key card, the receptionist who had noted the details added, "Thank you Ms Anapova, you are on the fourth floor, room 407. Breakfast is from 6:30 a.m. to 9:30 a.m. The lift is over here to your right. Oh, and by the way, you will need to insert your room card in the lift to access your floor. Have a pleasant night."

They entered the room and sank down on the beds. Wesley's eyes were like saucers as he stared at his surroundings. He had never seen or imagined anything such as a room like this in his life. In many ways Celia was almost as disoriented herself. Things were not as foreign to her as they were to her small son, but she still struggled to forage in her consciousness for any moment when she had experienced the comparative luxury of an environment like this.

"Celia," Olga said once they had calmed Wesley down a little and could talk. "I have a million things to tell you but most are not for now. Suffice to say I have got your passport and all your papers."

"But how?" interrupted Celia, totally amazed."

"I said it's 'not for now'. We both know how late it is and how tired we all are. I'll put you in the picture tomorrow." And then looking down at her watch continued, "Well later today to be precise. I'll explain it all then I promise."

When everyone had washed and showered and Wesley had been settled, Olga and Celia climbed into their respective beds. But before Olga switched out the light she reached for the bedside phone and dialled 0 for reception. When the phone was picked up at the other end, Olga said, "Hello, this is room 407. Can I order a room service breakfast for three for 6:30 a.m. please?" There was a slight pause as the details were registered and affirmed and then Olga said, "Thank you" and returned the receiver to its cradle.

Celia had already extinguished her light and drawn the luxurious Egyptian cotton sheets around her shoulders in absolute delight but when she heard what Olga had said on the phone, she sat up again and switched the light back on."

"Olga, what was that about? Why room service but most of all, why have you arranged for us to be woken so early? After everything that has gone on today we need a lie-in."

"I ordered room service," responded Olga, "because the restaurant would be far too overwhelming for Wesley. Surely you see that we have to ease him into the hustle and bustle of a place like this? Think back to what it was like for you the first time you left the flat - and you are an adult. We don't know whether it is going to be a scary or exciting experience for Wesley - probably a mixture of both - but we have to take that in mind, don't we? Apart from that, although this is not the first place that those looking for us will be thinking of, we should not take more chances than we have to. They have eyes all over the city."

Celia thought for moment and then said, "I am sorry, I see the need for room service, but what's with the 6:30 a.m. breakfast?"

"We need to be awake by 6:30 because we need to contact Angelika. I am sure you must have a contact number, have you? In one way we could phone her now as no one will be paying her a visit at this time of night - but tomorrow is a different thing. We will have to warn her first thing."

"But…. " began Celia.

"But nothing," retorted Olga. "I'll explain tomorrow."

They should not have concerned themselves about an alarm call. Wesley had been up and running around the room well before six. Exactly as ordered, the knock on the door came and a shining chrome trolley was wheeled into the room.

"Right," said Olga, seemingly used to a disposition of command and being aware that Celia really did not appear to complain. "Let's eat before we talk and then we will get down to serious business. I have a feeling that this is going to be a day that neither of us will ever forget."

When they had finished eating and had wheeled the trolley out into the corridor, Olga recounted all the events of the few days that had passed since they had last seen one another. She started with the assault on the gates, continued with the subterfuge at the restaurant and went on to the story of the break-in at the Kuznetsov's residence. She then concluded, as she drew the yet fully unopened parcel towards her, with the acquisition of the money.

Celia had been sitting with open-mouthed incredulity throughout the entire monologue, for the most part, her hands up to her cheeks in utter amazement. She had not interrupted. She had not said a word.

Olga struggled with the parcel. Only the edge had been partially uncovered enough for her to be able to pay the cab driver and cover the cost of their hotel stay. She had removed a few 100 euro notes but when the package was fully opened, they saw to their absolute amazement, that these at the edge had been in the minority. The vast proportion consisted of 500 euro notes. Olga had never seen a single note of such a high denomination in her life or even knew that such a note existed. Had they been able to check the internet at that moment they would have discovered that in 2010 precisely 594,833,600 were in circulation. When they looked down at what lay before them, they realised that they must have had notes to the value of over 250,000 euros right there in their possession. They stared in absolute disbelief. Wesley followed their gaze and just saw stacks of bits of paper.

"We will talk about this later," said Olga. "First, we have to warn Angelika. It's 7:15 a.m. She will be up by now. Do you have that number Celia? Obviously you should be the one to talk to her."

They briefly discussed a plan of action and mutually reached a decision. Celia was just about to lift up the hotel phone, when Olga gently checked the progress of her arm and then extending her mobile towards her, saying, "I think it would be safer to use this."

Angelika answered after about five rings and as she did not recognise the caller ID, said in a nervous and hesitant voice, "Hello, who is this?"

"Hi Angelika, this is Tania. How are you?"

"I am fine Tania," came the faltering reply. "It's a bit early, are you and Wesley OK?"

"Yes, we are fine. Angelika, do you remember that once you said to me the words, 'You have to get us out of this?'"

Angelika thought for a moment and then replied, "Well, yes I do but.."

"Then just listen closely Angelika. Today is the day!"

"What do you mean, today?"

"Angelika, you have to listen to me. You have to trust me and do precisely what I say. Will you do that?"

"Well yes, I suppose so but what…?"

"Listen Angelika. You may be in some danger and I want you and the children to pack everything that you need - the essentials that is - and leave the house within the hour if possible."

"But where will we go?"

"Don't worry about that now, just listen carefully. Do you have any money?"

"Yes a little but…"

"Right, as soon as you can, I want you and the children to get a cab and ask to be taken to the main railway station. When he drops you off I want you to look across the road and you will see a big hotel. Do you know the one I mean?"

"Yes, I have seen it," continued Angelika, somewhat flustered and confused.

"Right, well do not go into the hotel. I want you to look two blocks to the right and you'll see a coffee shop - one of the well known brands. Do you think you could be there by 9:30 a.m.?"

"Yes, I think so but…"

"Don't worry Angelika, everything is going to be OK but only if you work quickly. Do you have a mobile phone?"

"Yes, an old one, the 'pay as you go' type. I can't afford to use it much."

"Good, well make sure it is charged and when you get to the coffee shop, phone me on the number I am about to give you. Within fifteen minutes from then I will be with you.

Angelika made a note of the number.

"Now Angelika," Celia felt as if she was talking to a child but knew she needed to be precise. "Angelika, I know this may seem scary but try not to pass on any sense of fear to the children. Tell them they are about to go on a great adventure or something - or that you have a surprise for them. That usually works doesn't it?"

Celia was trying hard to put a note of cheerfulness and assurance in her own voice but was finding it difficult. She knew that Angelika was not used to 'big moments' or taking decisive actions of any kind at all. Most of her choices were made for her either by circumstances or by other people.

"So are we totally clear on that?" asked Celia.

"Yes, I think so. The coffee shop at 9:30 a.m."

"Good, I'll see you then. God bless and don't worry."

Celia pressed the 'end' button and passed the mobile back to Olga.

"No, you better keep it." Olga told her. "You'll need it when you meet her."

It was almost 10 a.m. before the mobile rang. Celia's heart had been pounding, wondering if those searching for her had got to Angelika first.

"Is that you Angelika? Are you at the coffee shop and are the children with you?"

"Yes I am here. We are all here."

"Fine, I'll be with you in just a few minutes."

When Celia entered the coffee shop she looked around and then noticed three anxious faces. The children had juices in front of them and Angelika was nursing what looked like a latte in her two hands - like someone trying to keep warm on a cold day - even though it was April.

"Hello aunty Tania, is Wesley with you?" A small voice asked as Celia approached the table.

"No, not today dear, though he will be sorry not to be able to play with you both," said Celia, glancing beyond the tables to a small section of the cafe that was set out as a children's play area.

"Angelika, good to see you." And pointing across the room said, "Do you think the children might go over there where we can keep an eye on them but still be able to talk?"

The children were gone before their mother could answer and then Celia met Angelika's gaze.

"Thank you for coming and doing as I asked. I know I have sprung so much on you out of the blue, as it were, but you have to trust me when I say that it was the only option that could possibly be taken."

Celia could see that Angelika's eyes looked as if they contained a hundred questions. Anticipating this, it was Celia who spoke first.

"I am going to ask that you let me talk to begin with. I know there are lots of things you need to know and I have no doubt at all that you must be worried - very worried indeed - but try and listen without interrupting while I give you all the background and then you can go on to ask all the questions you want at the end."

Angelika nodded her head in compliance.

"About twelve hours ago Wesley and I had to escape the flat. I won't go into any more detail now, as those facts don't affect you directly. We had no option and it was literally the only chance we would ever have. So we took it. I knew that you desperately wanted to get out of the clutches of these people too. Am I right?"

Angelika simply nodded her head in three sharp staccato movements.

"Right," continued Celia. "It was then clear that if it was 'now or never for me,' it was equally going to be 'now or never' for you as well."

Just one quick nod this time.

"I knew that as soon as they found that I had gone, they would be sure to question you, as you were almost the only contact I had with the outside world. You would not have been able to give them any answers because you did not know anything. However, they may not have believed you and you may have ended up getting hurt and apart from that, the children may have been in danger too."

No nods this time but it was evident that Angelika was taking in every word.

"That is what has brought us to this point," Celia continued.

It looked as if Angelika was about to say something and Celia had no doubt what it was likely to concern.

"Now I know you have no money, at least not an amount that you can live on, but do you have anywhere that you could stay? Are there family or friends with whom you could stay - someone who could accommodate you for perhaps just a few weeks?"

Angelika considered for a few moments but it was a shake of the head rather than a nod that ensured.

"Are you absolutely sure?" Celia asked, trying to conceal any desperation in her voice.

"What about a town that you know well and where you would feel safe for a while?"

Angelika thought again and then a half a smile came to her face.

"There might be a place," she began. "It is near a town where I once lived but it's a long way away from here - perhaps even 150 kilometres."

"What was it like?" asked Celia hopefully.

"Oh it was gorgeous. I told you that I came from a very poor background but this place was not very far away - so near in fact that we could cycle to it as children. Lots of tourists went there. We could never afford to live somewhere like that but it was a wonderful place to escape to from time to time. I wish now that those two," she paused and pointed across the room to her two children as they played blissfully oblivious to the importance of the conversation the two grown-ups were having.

"This sounds ideal," said Celia

"Ideal for what. Tania?"

"Ideal for you and the children to live. And by the way, you don't need to call me Tania any more. I have found out that my actual name is Celia."

"Honestly Tania... I mean Celia... is that your real name?"

"Yes, and I want you to listen very carefully to what I am now about to say."

As she spoke, Celia drew a large envelope from her bag and glanced around to see if she might be overheard, but by now the people who had been sitting on the two adjacent tables had left.

"Angelika, in this packet are three thousand euros."

Celia had selected all the lower denominations in Olga's packet. There was no way anyone was going to accept a 500 euro note from a poorly dressed woman without questioning how she might have acquired it, or wondering if it was genuine.

"You did not just say that?" exclaimed Angelika in disbelief. "I have never even seen more than a few hundred at one time - and that was a long time ago - but three thousand! Where did you get it from? And anyway I could not take it Tania, I mean Celia, because I could never pay it back!"

"You won't have to pay it back," said Celia. "You have worked like a slave for these people and been kept in poverty by them for ages. Look upon it as accumulated wages. Don't ask where it came from because I am not going to tell you. All you need to know is that, without them knowing, your employers have stumped up what they legitimately owe you. In fact, there is more to come but I knew that you would be nervous enough carrying even this amount around with you, let alone me giving you more. What I suggest is that when you leave here, you and the children go to the station down the road and get a train to as near to that town as you can. You may have to change once or even twice on the way. If there is no train link to your final destination, then you can certainly afford a cab, can't you?"

Celia glanced at her watch before continuing.

"I reckon if it's 150 km from here, and even allowing for changes, you will be there by early evening. So I suggest that you book a room for you and the children for a couple of days while you look for a more permanent apartment. Do you still have the mobile number I gave you this morning?"

Angelika looked into her purse and nodded.

"Right," said Celia. "As soon as you are settled I want you to ring me. When you do, I will arrange for a sum of money to be sent to you every month for at least the next two years."

When the children heard the sobs, they swivelled their heads towards the sound, and abandoning the toys, ran and instinctively flung their arms around the shoulders of their mother.

"What's wrong Mummy? Why are you crying? Please, Mummy, are you OK?"

Angelika hugged the two of them to her with all the strength she had.

"It's all right my little loves," Angelika said through her tears. "Your mummy is not crying because she is sad - everything is alright."

Eventually releasing them, she stood to her feet. Celia mirrored the action and they met in the aisle. This time it was Celia who she locked in her embrace and as Angelika's head rested on the taller woman's shoulder, her tears started all over again. After a moment or two Angelika pulled back and looked Celia straight in the eyes. "I will never be able to thank you enough for this. I have prayed for years that by some miracle I could free myself from their control but had begun to lose hope that it could ever happen. Today you have made it possible."

"Well, you know what the Bible says Angelika? There are times when it seems that God is silent but there are also times when God does something, 'exceedingly more than ever we could ask or imagine.' I think this might be one of those days for you."

Angelika and Celia hugged for a final time. Then Angelika reached down and held the two children in her embrace. Celia watched them leave in the direction of the train station. When they were almost out of sight, she watched as they paused, turned and gave her a final wave.

"Hello," he said raising his voice a little. "This is Damian Clarke. Can I help you?"

The voice at the other end was raised a notch for the same reason.

"Mr Clarke this is Olga Anapova."

Whether there was recognition at the other end or whether the man was thinking, she did not know.

"This is Olga Anapova - though you may remember me better as Priscilla."

There was another pause and then Olga heard a slight intake of breath on the line.

Marshalling his emotions as best as he could, Damian continued in the hope that no quiver in his voice could be detected. In measured tones he eventually answered.

"And what exactly do you want Ms Anapova? Why would you be calling me now or at any other time?"

"Mr Clarke, I can well understand your reticence to communicate with me at all after I abused your hospitality."

"Abused our hospitality?" said Damian, aware that the level of his voice was rising and his intonation was becoming something less than 'measured'.

"We offered hospitality, as you call it, to someone who we thought was vulnerable and in a measure of distress. Not to someone who had deceptively inveigled themselves in our home in order to spy on us and our friends."

Olga interrupted him.

"Mr Clarke, all I ask is that you give me just a few moments."

Damian was furious and was about to end the call. Olga sensed that this was her last chance and so almost shouted down the phone, "Celia is alive!"

Damian's finger was centimetres away from the red 'end call' button but as he heard Celia's name, he pulled the phone back to his ear.

"What did you just say?"

"I said, Celia is alive and I can prove it."

Over the next fifteen minutes Olga recounted her part in the story, her friendship with Celia - who she had known as Tania - right up to their escape within the past twenty four hours.

Within five minutes Damian had convinced himself that what he was hearing was true.

When eventually Olga had answered Damian's cascade of questions to the best of her ability, it was she who spoke next.

"Mr Clarke, I am sure that you will want to get on the phone to Jack straight away but there's another call that I think we both agree needs to be made and made very quickly. The people that nearly had Jack killed, and were responsible for Celia's injury and subsequent incarceration are still a threat to Celia's life and they are in this City turning over every stone to find us both. Frankly, if they discover where we are, everything could still be lost. Mr Clarke, when I shadowed you at Paddington station, one of the men that left the First Class lounge with you was a man called Poska. Am I right?"

"You are absolutely right," replied Damian, with not a little urgency in his voice.

"Well I suggest that if either you or Jack has a contact number for him, you need to get hold of him as soon as you possibly can and let him know that we are safe, at least for the moment, but how long that will last I cannot say. If you need to reach me you have got the name of our hotel and if you ask for room 407 they will put you through."

"Yes," said Damian, "I will certainly do that but I mean to call Jack first anyway - not just because he needs to know the news about Celia but because he is the only one with contact details for Poska. Of course, I am not entirely sure where Jack is at the moment - in Manchester, Scotland or elsewhere. I will obviously try all the numbers that I have that could be a means of getting hold of him. Thank you so much for getting in contact with me and by the way, now I realise the important part that you have played in Celia's safety to this point, is it OK if I call you 'Olga'?"

"Of course you may," Olga responded."

Olga put down the phone with a sigh of relief. Things had gone better than she had expected. There was another arrangement that she had made with Damian before the call had ended and there had been also one factor that she had purposely omitted from the account that she had given.

Jack joined his mother in the kitchen and was just reaching out for the kettle to make a pot of tea when the phone rang.

"It's OK I'll get it Sarah," a voice came from the lounge.

Elizabeth, Jack's aunt had been staying with her sister for some years and was by the phone.

"Hello, who am I speaking to?"

"It's Damian, Elizabeth, is Jack staying with you at the moment by any chance?"

"He is indeed Damian, in fact he is just in the other room with his mum. Do you want me to get him for you? But anyway, how are you and how is Sue?"

"We're both fine, thank you. Yes, I'd be grateful if you would pass the phone over to him, but listen Elizabeth, I know that this might sound strange, but could you make sure that you and Sarah are in the room as he takes the call?"

Elizabeth wondered at the strangeness of the request, did not ask further and called out, "Jack, it's Damian on the phone for you!"

Jack came out of the kitchen to the lounge as Elizabeth went in to see Sarah, who looked quizzically, as her sister appeared holding one finger over her lips and with her other hand, was waving Sarah towards her - beckoning her into the room.

"Hello, Damian, good to hear from you. Are you and Sue OK? What's the weather like down there?"

Jack looked up and was surprised to see his mother and aunt sitting together on the sofa across from him. Usually if he took a call they would slip away to give him space, assuming that the call may be work related.

"Are you sitting down?" Damian asked.

"I am actually," responded Jack. "I hope it's not terribly bad news though. Is there something wrong at one of the Centres? Don't keep me in suspense Damian, just spill it out."

The anxiety on Jack's face was now mirrored in the faces of the two older women sitting opposite him.

"Jack I have just had a call from that woman - you know the one who called herself Priscilla and stayed under false pretences?"

"Good heavens," interrupted Jack. "Why on earth would she be calling you ? What is she after this time?"

"Jack, I am going to say this slowly, so get ready for some earth-shattering news. You are hardly going to believe what I am about to say. She says that, not only is Celia alive and well but that she and her are together right now at this very moment!"

Jack responded first with a gasp of ecstasy, followed immediately by a sense of sheer panic.

"Damian, what is going on? Are you telling me that woman is making a ransom demand for Celia?"

At the sound of Celia's name, the two woman opposite, looked at one another, rose from the settee and edged towards both Jack and the phone, as if by shortening the distance it would in some way make the situation clearer. Elizabeth's arm was around Sarah's shoulder and Sarah had her hand clasped to her mouth.

"No it's nothing like that at all Jack, don't worry on that point. Celia is safe at least for the moment - but I will come to that in a minute. The woman's real name is Olga - if you remember, Poska told us that at Paddington station. Apparently she has become, not only Celia's closest friend, but the architect of Celia's escape."

"Escape?" said Jack. "What do you mean 'escape'?"

Over the next few minutes Damian passed on everything that he knew and ended up with Olga's request that he update Poska with the situation as urgently as possible. His mother and aunt were not a little surprised that when the call had ended, instead of immediately explaining to them what had happened, he had reached into his inside pocket for his mobile, scrolled down his speed-dial and pressed a number.

There was a tentative knock on the door marked 407 and instinctively Olga looked across at Wesley and signalled that he should not make a sound. Rising from her chair she tiptoed to the door and looking through the security spy hole in the door, confirmed it was Celia, lifted the latch and let her in. Wesley jumped off the bed where he had been watching TV, recognising who it was, ran to her and gave his mother a hug.

"I have missed you Mummy," Wesley wailed.

"Goodness me," responded Celia. "I've only been gone for a couple of hours. What's all the fuss? What's all this about? You had auntie Olga with you didn't you?"

"I know, I know," came the plaintive reply, "but I still missed you!"

"So how did it go?" asked Olga, as Wesley climbed back on the bed and returned to his cartoons

"It was emotional, let's say that," replied Celia. "In fact we both were in floods of tears before she left."

"Left for where?" asked Olga.

"It seems she knew a place that would be safe about three or four hours away by train, so she's hopefully on her way there by now. She's going to send us an address when she's settled and I said that we would send her something, as we arranged, on a monthly basis. She was ecstatic as you might imagine. It could not have happened without you Olga, you know that don't you? At first you seemed almost indifferent to her situation and then you ended up being the means of changing the entire trajectory of her future. I ended up just being the courier."

"I don't know about that," replied Olga. "But the money she will be receiving over the next couple of years is strictly hers anyway. She has been kept in emotional and physical bondage almost as much as the women those beasts are trafficking - though perhaps her situation was not quite as bad. Nevertheless, that money belongs to her and we will make sure that she gets it."

Olga looked across to the little boy on the bed to make sure that he was not listening. When she saw he was fully engrossed in his programme, she put the question that was in her mind to Celia.

"You know, when you think of all the pain that so many people are put through by people like them, I am amazed, to be frank with you, that you can still believe in a loving God."

"Hang on a minute," Celia responded to her friend. "I thought that you believed in God yourself Olga."

"Well there are times when I am not so sure. When I see the faith my mother has - and particularly the transformation in my father when he started to believe - I think I do. But then, when I consider all the trouble there is in the world and the fact that, if there was an all-powerful God that he could stop it.... well it's then that I find myself all the way back at square one again. Do you see what I mean?"

Celia paused before she answered. It wasn't that she was dizzy - her head was not spinning but her mind was certainly racing and she felt her heart was pounding out of her chest. At that moment, she saw in her mind's eye, the man she now knew to be Jack sitting with her in that cafe that she had once recognised in the old part of Tallinn. What was the name of the place? That's it 'Raekoja Plats'. She could see it as if it had happened yesterday. Not only that but she saw Jack asking almost the very same question that Olga was posing to her now.

"Celia, are you alright? I hope that I have not upset you by asking."

"No, it's alright, really it is," said Celia, coming back from what Olga must have thought was almost a trance-like state. "I'm sorry Olga, what was it that you were saying?"

"Oh it doesn't matter - really it doesn't."

"No, please go on," requested Celia. "Something about a loving God and how he could allow suffering and all that. Am I right?"

"Yes but.." began Olga.

"No, it's a fair enough question. I am sure lots of people must ask it. I have not got a clue who said it but somewhere in the back of my mind - and you know what my mind's like, I seem to recollect that someone said. 'How could anyone believe in soap when there were so many people in the world with dirty faces.' It's a silly answer in a way but I tend to get the point, don't you? I suppose it's to do with recognising people's responsibility when it comes to justice - as well as God's part in the equation. It's all to do with the freewill that He has given us and that He does not control us as if we were robots. What kind of world would that be like anyway?"

Olga thought for a moment. She had been trying to listen to her friend's response, while at the same time, hoping that Celia had not been noticing the fact that she had been glancing regularly at her watch.

"Yes, I see what you mean," said Olga. "But it's a bit like those conversations we used to have at your flat when subjects liked this cropped up. I listen to you answer and lots of times I can see where you are coming from. I would even go so far as to say that I find myself agreeing with you more often than not. It's just that there always seems to be a gap - something missing, I don't know what it is."

"Gap's a good word actually," answered Celia, wondering why her friend always seemed to be looking at her watch. "It is a gap actually - a fifteen centimetre gap."

"A what?" responded Olga, questioningly.

"It's the distance between your head and your heart. You can understand it but at the moment at least, you can't feel it yet."

It was then that the phone rang.

"Could you get that Celia?" said Olga, with a little too much enthusiasm in her voice. "I think I'll take Wesley for a stroll around the corridors. We won't go far. I think he needs to be out of this place for a while. It will help him to acclimatise himself."

The phone was still ringing and Celia looked between it and Olga who was pulling a surprised Wesley from his cross-legged position on the bed, towards the door. Within seconds Olga had left the room and Celia looked back towards the phone, deciding that had she better answer it.

"Good afternoon, this is reception. Is that room 407 booked in the name of Ms Anapova?"

"Yes it is," responded Celia. "But I am afraid she isn't here at the moment. She shouldn't be long though. Shall I get her to contact you when she returns?"

"I have an international call for someone called Celia. That would not be you by any chance?"

"Yes it is but…"

"Thank you, then I will put it though."

"Hello?"

It was a man's voice at the other end.

"Hello, could I speak to Celia please?"

"Yes, this is Celia, how can I help you?"

There was a pause before the caller continued.

"Celia, this is Jack."

This time Celia's head did go dizzy. For a moment she thought she was going to pass out. Then she realised she had a phone in her hand and pulling herself together, sat down and drew it back to her ear.

"Celia, are you still there?"

"Yes, Jack, I'm here. It's just such a shock hearing your voice after all this time. How did you know how to reach me? I still can't believe…"

"Olga phoned this morning - actually she didn't phone me, she phoned Damian and Damian phoned me. I understand you were out somewhere. She told Damian everything and Damian rang me. Between the three of us we decided to set up this call.

Celia's mind rewound to the scene a few minutes earlier and recaptured the image of her friend continually consulting her watch. She had set this all up and had ensured that when the call came there would be total privacy in which she could receive it. How she loved that woman!

"My head's in a whirl if I'm honest, I must sound so silly," said Celia apologetically.

"Not at all," answered Jack. "It must have been a massive shock for you and actually it's been something of a day for me too, given I only heard that you were both alive and well just a few hours ago. I'm staying at my mother's home here in Scotland."

Jack paused realising that Celia would still be struggling with memory issues and she probably had no idea at all what he was talking about.

"Scotland?" Celia said. "I thought your parents lived here in Tallinn."

She was amazed that she had remembered even that and then she recalled that Jack's father, the person that astonishingly she had named Wesley after, was now dead.

"My mother moved to Scotland after my father passed away and she is living up here in Scotland with her sister, my aunt Elizabeth. I stay partly here and partly in Manchester, where I rent an apartment."

She noticed that he had said 'I' and not 'we' but she had to be totally sure. Several years had passed since they had been together and Jack - she could see his face and form now as if he was there in front of her - was a handsome and attractive man and well....

"Jack, I hardly know how to ask this."

There was a pause at the other end of the line. Jack had wondered if his wife, believing him to be dead, had met someone else. But when Olga had related the confinement she had been subjected to, he did not even need to ask, he sensed immediately what his wife was struggling with."

"No Celia, there is no-one else. There has never been any one. To be absolutely honest, I don't think that there ever could be anyone else."

It was not that there was silence on the end of the phone because there wasn't. Jack could hear the sobs of the woman he loved, even though there was over a thousand miles of distance between them.

He did not interrupt for a while.

For Celia's part she knew that her emotions had been rising like one of those geysers - subterraneous streams, that had been kept captive until they burst forth through the earth's surface. What she was experiencing now was a mixture of shock, relief, weariness, gratitude and anticipation. She realised that Jack was giving her some space and she loved him all the more for it.

"It's OK Jack, I'm here, I am fine. We are both a little overwhelmed aren't we? I know I am."

"Of course we are," Jack reassured her. "But listen, you get some rest. We will leave it there for now. We will have plenty of time to talk soon and a whole life together to look forward to. It seems Olga has booked you both into the hotel for a few more days. I think that is a good decision. Make sure that you stay there and stay safe. I am going to get the first flight I can to Estonia. I will be with you in just a few days time. I promise. Incidentally, I should have asked, how are the two of you for money? Is there anything I..."

"No, we are fine on that score Jack, I promise," said Celia, a mite too quickly, she later thought!. "But it was thoughtful of you to ask."

Jack had not mentioned Poska or any other calls that he had made. He knew that Olga was keenly tuned in to the danger she and Celia were still in, but he sensed somehow that Celia was not as acutely aware of it as Olga was. In one way that was good, he thought to himself, and in another, perhaps not.

Olga had placed her ear to the door, not to listen but to know when it was appropriate for her to come back in. She had the key card with her, so did not have to knock. When her friend came in, Celia rushed over to her and held her in the tightest of embraces. Wesley looked up with an air of indifference, climbed back on the bed, picked up the remote and switched on the TV. *Women were strange creatures, - not like boys,* he thought to himself.

Two Days Earlier

When the Kuznetsov's returned to their house it was already dark. As he neared his drive he fumbled in the centre of the console for the key fob to open the gates before he realised two things. The first was that he had flung the fob out of the window in frustration when the gates had not opened, as he had assumed that it was faulty. The second, was that he did not have any gates anyway as they had been removed. This meant of course that he could not get the electronic doors on the garage to work either as he had no fob - but no problem - he would leave the car in the drive until the morning. Anyway, if he needed to, he could always open the garage doors manually from the inside once he was in the house. *Will I do that? - No,* he thought to himself, *too tired and can't be bothered, I'll just leave it where it is.*

It had certainly been a good meal. When the sommelier had brought the wine list he had checked that their benefactor - should he refer to that person as their 'gate-crasher' - had supplied sufficient funds for them to select a decent vintage. It appeared that they had. As they had chatted over the meal, they still could not quite make it out. If the perpetrator had got away from the scene, why should they bother to contact them at all? They could never be identified. If the boot had been on the other foot, thought Kuznetsov, hell would freeze over before he would extend such a gesture of magnanimity. He paused for a minute to wonder why he had chosen to use the word 'gesture'.

They entered the front door and then, having unarmed the security system with the code, they both made their way towards their bedroom. Normally he let his wife retire first while he selected a 'night-cap' but they had both eaten and drunk enough for one evening.

They were in bed, and his wife had already dropped off to sleep. However, he simply could not rest. It was that little word 'gesture' again. He could not get it out of his mind. Something was wrong. He did not know what it was. He needed to settle the matter one way or another or he would be tossing and turning all night.

At that point he did not realise that he would be virtually up all night anyway.

He slipped out of bed and reached for the silk dressing gown draped over an adjacent chair. The first port of call needed to be the safe. He entered the room where it was housed, removed the oil painting that covered it, saw that the green flashing light indicated that it had not been tampered with, replaced the painting and wandered off to reconnoiter elsewhere. He commenced with the downstairs windows and saw nothing out of place. He checked all exterior doors and discovered each intact. He re-climbed the stairs, crossed the landing, and checked the windows in every room on the second floor.

So if no one had broken in, why was he still worried?

Though it was late the restaurant would be open for at least a couple of hours yet. At the time he had not thought to ask the identity of the person who had covered the cost of the meal. Why should he have? What difference did it make? But perhaps he should have done, he thought to himself. He was outside his study and so thought he would make the call from there. He switched on the light. He had already been in the room earlier and made a cursory glance towards the windows. There had been nothing amiss here either. But it was when he walked to the other side of his desk that he saw it.

Mrs Kuznetsov was a notoriously heavy sleeper and his wife had also been at the wrong end of the verbal invective of her husband when he was in a rage. However, the booming sound of unfettered expletives that emanated from somewhere in the house, was something she had never experienced before. The noise, she concluded, would have awakened the dead.

Kuznetsov hurled the remains of the already damaged drawer away from the desk, spilling its contents on the carpet. He knew exactly what should have been there and so he immediately saw what was missing. His gun was there, as were some inconsequential papers. But the passports and the documents that related to them, were gone. He rummaged around the debris on the floor in an accelerating frenzy to find that he was also short of over two hundred and fifty thousand euros.

It was as clear as day that whoever had done this had some connection with the Edwards woman and her kid. They could not have done it personally, so who had? If she had not been responsible for this, then there was little doubt that she would at least know who had. Normally he would have called in all the 'muscle' that he needed but he had no time for that. He wanted answers tonight. And answers he would get, whatever he needed to do to her or her brat, to get them.

He returned to the bedroom, shouting an incoherent volley of abuse as he attempted to get dressed. Mrs Kuznetsov was sitting up in bed with the duvet pulled around her neck, as if by doing so she could fend off the tirade that was coming, unfairly, in her direction. She was still sitting there in that terrified posture, when minutes later, she heard a car accelerate out of the drive.

Kuznetsov guessed the woman would be in bed by now, so there was no need to speed. He had never visited her place in person but knew where all the 'safe houses' were located and he knew which one housed the English woman and the child.

He was less than a kilometre away and knew that after the next turn he would be there. Cutting the corner he found himself on the wrong side of the road and pulled back heavily on the wheel, only narrowly missing a taxi coming in the opposite direction. Irrationally he swore through the closed window of his Mercedes in the direction of a cab that had already passed him.

Early the next morning Kuznetsov was seated, surrounded by some of the henchmen that he had not thought necessary to call the previous night. None of them spoke and certainly no-one referred to the fact that their dishevelled employer looked as though he had not slept for a week

"I don't care what it costs or who gets hurt! This problem has to be sorted very quickly indeed. You bozos may think that you are hard but you are ballerinas compared to the people above me who are going to be unhappy if this leaks out - and leak out it inevitably will. This is infinitely bigger than a woman, a kid and the loss of a lot of money."

Of the five men who faced him, none would meet his eye. Some fidgeted nervously. One rubbed his fingers across his moustache and another looked down at his brown shoes.

"I've been awake most of the night as you all might have noticed. Apart from the people in this room, there are only two other links to the Edwards woman. One we can discount. She is the young widow we had to 'babysit' the kid while the English woman was working for us. She hardly knows what day of the week it is and certainly could never plan an operation like this. However, if this is not cleared up in the next forty eight hours, then one of you will have to pay her a visit anyway. No, the only one in the frame right now, is Olga Anapova. There was a contract out on her after her father died. Someone must have tipped her off. I don't know how. But she was not even at her father's funeral - the place at which the job to terminate her should have been executed. We can't use her mother as leverage as she has flown too and could be anywhere in the country by now - or even abroad. I have absolutely no doubt that she is the key to all of this and she has to be found. When she is found we can be sure that the woman and the boy will be found too. All three of them have to be eliminated - the women know too much. Remember, Anapova can identify all our operations since she has been with us, and the English woman, I can hardly believe I am saying this, has had access to all our primary spreadsheets."

No one had uttered a word at this point but then the one that Celia would have only known as 'brown shoes' and had began taking a liking to the child they called 'Wesley' asked, "Does the little boy need to be dealt with too…I mean..?"

"Of course the kid needs to be dealt with too," Kuznetsov snapped. "There can be no loose ends this time."

Kuznetsov was disinclined to mention the issue of the gates and the subsequent meal. It would make him look an absolute idiot in front of his men and that would not be good for discipline.

Kuznetsov decided to visit the Maison D'Or as soon as it was open. The Maitre D' was talking to some early guests and so he waited until he was free. When he saw that the diners had been allocated to a waiter and were being steered towards their table, he walked forward.

"Ah, Mr Kuznetsov, how are you? And how is Mrs Kuznetsov this evening? Is she not with you?" said the Maitre D' as he glanced across.

Kuznetsov thought to himself how amazing it was that these people were able to remember names - even of people they had met only perhaps once or twice.

"If it is a table for tonight Mr Kuznetsov, I regret that will be not be possible, even for you I am afraid, - we are fully booked - not a table to spare."

"No it's nothing like that. It's just… information that I need."

"Information sir? Information of what sort? If it's concerning future availability then the front desk - the desk you passed on your way in, that's the person to see."

"No it's not that… it's er…. well, can I confide in you? You see my understanding is that someone approached you and generously covered the cost of the excellent meal we enjoyed at your establishment last evening."

"Yes I think you knew that already, sir."

"Yes, of course I did," muttered Kuznetsov.

"Alright, I can do it, but it may be twenty four hours before I can get anything to you."

"A day will be fine," said Kuznetsov. "But please do not keep me waiting any longer than that. You need to let me know the moment you find something out. You know how to reach me."

It was in fact late that same night that Kuznetsov took the call.

"Right what have you got?" barked Kuznetsov, discarding either preamble or pleasantry.

"The card was used as you know for the Maison D'Or. The next and only other time it has been used was for the amount of five euros."

"Five euros," barked Kuznetsov, before the caller could finish his sentence. "Who the hell uses a credit card for five euros?"

"You would do so when registering your card at a hotel. It is a nominal amount that is refunded or deducted from the invoice when checking out," came the reply.

For once in his life Kuznetsov was momentarily speechless.

"Are you telling me you have an address?"

"Yes, right here in the City. I'll text you the details right away."

"Remind me what date it is today?" asked Kuznetsov.

"It's Thursday sir."

"I know it's Thursday you fool, I said what date."

"Oh, it's the 1st Mr Kuznetsov. I'm sorry, the first of April."

Kuznetsov ended the call and waited for the text. When it arrived he noticed it even included a room number - his informant had been busy. He punched in some other numbers and when the call was picked up, all the person at the other end heard was, "It's me, we've got them. We will finish them for good tomorrow."

Celia and Olga 2010 May 2nd

Celia did not think she would sleep a wink the night following her call from Jack but in fact she slept well and was only woken by a knocking on the door that heralded the breakfast trolley. Wesley had been up before everyone as usual but Olga had insisted that he should not disturb his mother and to his credit, the little boy had complied.

When the trolley was back out in the corridor, and Wesley had taken his usual position in front of the TV, Olga whispered across to Celia to say that they needed to talk and signalled towards the bathroom. They were all living on top of one another - something that Celia and Wesley were used to but Olga was not. That neither of them had become tetchy or irritable was evidence of the strength of their friendship. However, there were occasions when they needed to conduct adult conversations outside the parameters of little ears.

"What's the matter?" asked Celia, when they were out of ear-shot.

"There are some things we need to talk through and address soon," began Olga.

"Like what for example?"

"Well, for starters, what the next step is," said Olga. "I have been making all the decisions up to now and you have been just tagging along with everything. It's not that I am complaining, but the landscape's changed now hasn't it? It's not just you, me and Wesley any more. After tomorrow morning when Jack flies in …."

"You mean he's coming tomorrow?" said Celia excitedly. "You never told me that!"

"That's my point entirely," responded Olga. "He's your husband and yet it was me that got a call from reception just after you got your head down, to ask if I would go down to reception to pick up a message that had been left. "Is that room 407 under the name of Ms Olga Anapova?" they asked.

"Why didn't you tell me last night?" asked Celia.

"I did not tell you last night because it had been a massive day for you and you needed your sleep. If I had told you, all the adrenalin in the world would have kicked in. That's why we are talking now."

"That was kind and thoughtful of you Olga but I still can't see the problem."

"Can't see the problem!" intoned Olga, in something between a shout and a whisper. "Jack is coming tomorrow and Wesley does not even know he has a father. Have you thought about that?"

Celia leaned back against the towel rail.

"You're right Olga. You are absolutely right. Things just moved so fast yesterday. Obviously, it was in my mind but probably because I did not know when Jack was arriving."

Celia thought for a moment.

"But at least Jack knows he has a son - you would have mentioned that to Damian when you spoke to him on the phone, right?

"Of course he doesn't know," Olga yelled in frustration. "That's not for me to say - you're his wife. I'm not the person to tell him news like that am I?"

"Mummy, auntie Olga, are you all right?" whimpered a small voice the other side of the bathroom door.

"Yes dear, auntie Olga and I are fine," Celia called out. "We're just having a little talk. We will be back with you soon - just enjoy your programme love."

"So Jack doesn't know?" Celia said to herself more than Olga.

"No, he doesn't," Olga affirmed.

"I am not absolutely sure, but his plane gets in around two, so I assume it will be mid afternoon by the time he deplanes, gets through customs and gets over here. I'll obviously make myself scarce when he arrives. You need to meet him on your own - and I mean on your own. You can't have Jack walking in, having thought you were dead for the past four years and then seeing you and a little boy. I'll keep Wesley with me while you talk and then bring him up to you later."

"That's a great idea," agreed Celia.

"You see, I'm still making the decisions Celia," said Olga. "You've got to get used to me not being around very soon. You see that don't you?"

"But what am I going to wear to meet him?" asked Celia.

"There you go again - can't you hear yourself? He won't care what you are wearing - why should he - all he wants to see is you, you silly girl!"

There was a tap on the door followed by, "Mummy, Mummy, can I come in, I want the toilet?"

Celia opened the door and she and Olga came back in the room. Wesley lifted his arms to be picked up and Celia hugged him close. Somehow the need for the bathroom had been forgotten.

"I tell you what Celia, I need some fresh air, so I think I am going out for a stroll." Then looking across at Wesley and back at her friend, she winked and said, "It'll give you some time to have a chat with that little man over there."

"You won't be going far will you? I mean, there will be people out everywhere looking."

"No, I won't be wandering too far at all, I promise. I think I'll pop over to the station, buy a couple of magazines from the news stand and then grab a coffee or something. That will do me for the rest of the morning. I tell you what, why don't you order room service for noon and add a roast beef and horseradish sandwich for me to whatever you want for you and Wesley. I'll be back by then.

Olga used the stairs rather than the lift. She had been used to regular exercise and during the last couple of days, she had done little else other than sit and eat. In hotels like this all stairways eventually ended up at reception. She scanned the room and headed towards the revolving door at the main entrance.

As she walked forward, she sensed there was something that she felt was not quite right. Whenever she entered a room for the first time, especially if she was on an assignment, she always looked to see where the exits were - how many there were and how accessible. But she was leaving and not entering, so why was she worrying? And anyway, she had been through the lobby a number of times. What was it? Something was odd - but nothing was lodging in her consciousness. Perhaps she was being paranoid, after all, the past few days had been the most stressful of her entire life, why wouldn't she feel paranoid?

Olga walked over to the station concourse where she knew there would be both newsagents and coffee shops. She bought the magazines that she had promised herself and was on her second cup of coffee when she glanced down at her watch. It was 11:40 a.m. She needed to be heading for the door soon she thought. She had promised to be back by noon and did not want Celia to worry.

It was then that everything fell into place. That is what had been wrong - the doors. When she had entered the lobby from the stairwell, there had been the usual flurry of activity. Bell boys were pushing gilt-metalled suit carrier's on wheels, waitresses and hotel staff were scurrying backwards and forwards, some guests with suitcases next to them were seated, waiting for the taxis they had ordered to arrive. There was also the usual line of people at reception, either checking in or checking out.

But it was the doors - not just the doors to the street but the doors to other parts of the hotel and the doors to the lifts. She saw it now, but it had not registered earlier. Every door had some stationery person near by it. Mostly men but there had been one or two women too - and for some reason they fitted neither the profile of either guest or staff.

Olga threw her magazines to one side. Initially she had in mind to pass them on to Celia but that was the least of her concerns now. She raced at full speed from the coffee shop and along the road and did not slow down until she got to the steps of the hotel. If the people who had been there almost two hours ago were still in the same position something terrible was about to happen. There they were - every one of them - still in the same place. But what could she do other than make her way to the room? However, if she did that she would be as vulnerable as Celia and Wesley and they would all be trapped.

At that moment another thing occurred to her. The people on the doors could not be with Kuznetsov, as she knew all his men by sight and most of them by name. So, if they were not with him, who were they with? Olga looked at her watch again - 11:51 a.m. And then to her horror she realised that Celia would be opening the door to room service in under ten minutes time. She turned to a man nearest the revolving door and yelled, "If you are with Poska, follow me and follow me now!"

He looked with a startled expression at the slim brunette but then hearing the name 'Poska' his training kicked in under a second. No civilian would know that name.

Olga was already racing to the stairwell and the man was following her. It was mayhem in the lobby. The others in Poska's team saw the first agent sprint forward and they picked up the chase and headed in the same direction. Most people in the lobby just stood around looking dazed and confused. Others, sensing something was afoot, strode purposefully towards the exit.

Olga was taking the stairs at speed but the taller and fitter agent was taking the stairs two at a time and had soon overtaken her.

"The fourth floor!" Olga screamed to his advancing back, "look out for a waiter!"

The agent emerged from the stairwell to the fourth floor and looked along the maroon carpeted passageway. A man in a white jacket and black trousers was standing by a serving trolley, his hands poised to rap on the door.

"Freeze now and stand back - move away from the door! Do what I say right now," the agent shouted.

The 'waiter' whirled around in disbelief. At the same time, he pulled back the pristine white linen cloth that covered the trolley and from it grabbed a Glock 17 with a silencer fitted. He swung it round towards the agent. But it was too late. Bullets were already in motion in his direction. There was a double tap, two quick successive shots from the agent's pistol - and the assailant was down.

By this time Olga had caught up and had entered the passage just as the man had fallen. Fearful that Celia should come to the door with Wesley in tow, she raced towards the man who was down, gave a flying kick to the trolley that blocked her entrance to the door. It clattered down the hallway bumping the sides of the wall until it came to a final stop. She spread-eagled her body against the door as if protecting it from all on-comers and yelled, "Celia it's me, Olga, whatever you do, stay inside and keep Wesley with you. Do not open the door until I tell you to do so." *So much for not ordering Celia around and giving her space to think for herself*, she mused, as her body relaxed and she realised that Celia had heard her and was complying.

There were around eight agents in the passageway now. Most of whom were encouraging back into their rooms the guests who had come to their doors to see what all the commotion was about. The agent responsible for bringing the attacker down was on his phone and would be arranging for the body to be removed. When he had finished the call, Olga explained who she was and asked if she could go into her room and offer comfort and some explanation to the woman the agents had been assigned to protect. She was asked for identification and said that her passport was in the safe in the room. But when she pulled her credit card out of her bag and he saw the name 'O.Anapova', he was happy to let her proceed. The agents had been given the names of the occupants of the room and had been told to keep a low profile - far too low a profile it had turned out. They had not expected the tentacles of the organisation to stretch so far into the fabric of the hotel as they obviously had. Someone knew that a food order had been made and the time it was to be delivered, so they expected to find a second body before they left - that of the legitimate member of staff who was commissioned with the job of delivering the food.

"I have just spoken to Mr Poska on the phone to report on what has just taken place," said the agent, addressing Olga. "He has asked that you settle yourself in your room for the remainder of the day - to the extent that that is possible for you to 'settle' after all this of course. He will come in person to talk with you and Mrs Troughton at 10 a.m. tomorrow if you could make yourself available for that. It will not be appropriate for him to come to your room, so you will be telephoned from reception when he arrives. We will arrange with the management for a small conference room to be set aside for the purpose. Good afternoon Ms Anapova and thank you for alerting us to the threat as you did. Had you not intervened, both Mrs Troughton and her little boy would most certainly be dead."

"Very well," responded Olga. "But you need to be aware, if you are not already, that a man called Kuznetsov is behind this." As she said this, Olga reached for her purse, took out a pen, and wrote down his address before handing it to the agent.

When Olga entered the room she found Celia sitting on the bed, enfolding Wesley protectively in her arms. "It's over," Olga said as she approached them. "Everything is over. We are safe. We can all relax for the first time in a long time."

"But what happened out there?" asked Celia, shaken. "I heard shots."

"Olga looked at the wide-eyed little boy now hugging his mother.

"I'll tell you later. The people who intervened out there were Poska's men." And then she realised that Celia would not have a clue what she was talking about.

"Do you remember I told you that I had been following Jack without knowing he had anything to do with you?"

Celia nodded.

"Well, on one of those occasions I trailed him to Paddington. He was with Damian, who you know about and some other people. One of those people was a man called Poska, someone already known to

Jack. This man is the head of a 'special unit' right here in Tallinn. Jack would have alerted him to the fact that you might be in danger and he had stationed people at all the exits. Presumably they were there, so that if either of us left the hotel, we would be followed from a distance and therefore protected. What no one seemed to have taken on board was that someone could infiltrate the hotel as they did. And of course, they could hardly have a guard standing outside our door or in the corridor - they would stick out like a sore thumb and have the guests in the other rooms asking questions. However, in retrospect, that may not have been such a bad idea. I think that when they do a review on what has just taken place, Poska is going to be less than pleased and there will be a lot of explaining to be done. I imagine that right now one of the agents will be speaking to the manager and I guess there will be a lot of activity outside our door that does not need to concern us. I don't know about you Celia, but I am hungry. If we can hold on for an hour or so we can go down to the hotel restaurant. There won't be a need for room service any more, thank goodness."

"That's one good thing," said Celia, noticeably more relaxed. "Anyway, even though I know things are safe, it will be some time before I am comfortable to open the door to any one with a trolley."

"Oh, there is just one more thing," said Olga remembering. "Tomorrow morning at ten the man I told you about, Poska, is coming to the hotel. We will be meeting him individually in a room downstairs. That is a good thing if you think about it, because the other one of us can keep an eye on that little chap," she said, pointing over to Wesley with a smile.

"Well tomorrow is certainly going to be some day," said Celia. Poska in the morning and me meeting Jack in the afternoon!"

Poska 2010 May 3rd

Reception called the room at 9:45 a.m.

"There is a gentleman called Mr Poska who has booked the Baltic room on the first floor. He said he has an appointment and said that he would be grateful if Ms Anapova could find her way there in about fifteen minutes. Is that OK and shall I say that he is to expect you?"

Olga assured the receptionist that she was indeed happy with the arrangements.

A quarter of an hour later Olga knocked on the door and having heard the word 'Come!' entered the room.

The Baltic suite was the type used by business people when they wanted to hire a meeting room for a few hours or even for a day. A long table that could accommodate about twenty people filled the larger part of the room. There were writing pads and pens, that carried the hotel logo, positioned opposite each seat and small bowls of sweets and nuts were spaced along the centre. Bottles of still and sparkling water stood on a small separate table in a corner of the room.

Poska rose with a smile as Olga came in, extended his hand, and when they had greeted one another, motioned her to a chair opposite him at end of the table.

"Sorry this room is larger than we need but it was the only one I could get at such short notice. I wanted a place where we could talk in confidence," apologised Poska, in an attempt to put Olga at ease.

"I think we would both agree that there is a fair bit of ground we need to cover."

Olga was grateful for the measured informality. She realised, that given the people she had been associated with, any engagement she had with someone in this man's position, could mean that she could be in a great deal of trouble - with her perhaps even facing a prison sentence.

"I know that we have not met before, but I believe, that though this is the first time that I have seen you - you once saw me at a certain venue in London in the not too distant past, if I am not mistaken," continued Poska, with a wry smile.

Olga nodded somewhat sheepishly.

"Ms Anapova, or may I call you Olga?"

"Olga, yes by all means," she replied.

"Thank you. Olga, the first thing that I want you to do is to recount in your own words the events of yesterday. Try and cover every detail, however insignificant. What appears minutia to you, may be extremely significant as far as I am concerned. You need to be aware that this is an informal conversation. This is not being recorded - though I may occasionally jot things down as you speak. Statements may need to be given and signed at a police station at a later stage - that is not my department. You need to understand that you are not under arrest and that is why you have not been cautioned. Are you happy to proceed on that basis?"

"Yes," confirmed Olga. "I am."

Olga recounted everything she could remember about the previous day and Poska did not interrupt her. It was only when he assumed that she had concluded everything that she wanted to say, that he spoke.

"I have to say," Poska began, "the operation yesterday, from our perspective, left a very great deal to be desired. I would even go so far as to say to that it was only a little short of a shambles and had you not intervened when you did, the day may have concluded far differently than it did."

"Thank you sir," responded Olga.

"Now, I next want you to cover how you got involved with these people in the first place. You may, or may not know, that we have a fairly extensive file on you already but there are gaps in the picture that we have tried to put together that I trust you will be able to fill in. There are also other issues that I will want you to clarify. You may be aware that Jack and I - Jack Troughton that is - have met together on a number of occasions in the past and it was he, as I am sure you know, who was the person who made us aware of the most recent development. I mention this because he has also supplied us with valuable information about this criminal organisation and I am interested to see if your account parallels with his."

Over the next fifty minutes Olga shared openly and vulnerably her story, trying to leave nothing of importance out. Again Poska did not interrupt, apart from interjecting with some minor clarifying questions.

"I think the first thing that I want to thank you for Olga is for your frankness. I have noticed that you have not attempted to excuse yourself or gloss over areas in which, evidence would suggest, you may have been complicit with those who were controlling you. From what you have told me, there are several occasions when you have clearly operated well outside the parameters of the law - and there is no getting away from that. I have no doubt that other branches of our policing system in this country, and perhaps even abroad, will be taking that into consideration. Obviously, at this stage no promises can be made or assurances given - there are other people to be interviewed and a great deal of evidence to be sifted through, as you might imagine. Nevertheless, suffice to say, I will do all that I can to be of help. Mrs Troughton would not be out of her captivity without your involvement and as I said earlier, would not even be alive if you had not acted as you did yesterday."

Poska looked at his watch before continuing.

"I am not going to detain you a great deal longer. I need to speak to your friend Celia in the next few minutes and I know she will be meeting Jack here sometime later today, am I right?"

"Yes, Mr Poska," Olga said. "We think he will be here sometime late this afternoon."

"Ok then, let's proceed to the events surrounding your 'visit' to Mr Kuznetsov's residence."

Olga gulped hard and had no doubt that her interviewer had noticed the tension in her body language.

"Let's say," Poska continued, "you seem to have had an eventful couple of days."

Olga did her best to cover everything - the gates, the meal at the restaurant, the break-in, the removal of Celia and Wesley's documents - even the acquisition of the parcel containing the money.

Poska listened patiently and when Olga came to the account of the money, he asked where it was at the present time and she told him it was locked in the safe in their room.

"Right," said Poska "that's all for now and thank you again for the transparency of your answers. Perhaps you could ask Celia to join me."

Olga rose to go and just as her hand was on the handle of the door, she heard Poska's voice.

"Oh, just one more thing Olga before you go."

Olga wondered if this man could hear her heart pounding as loud as she could. *It was like in the films*, she thought, *it always seemed that the police, because that was really what he was at the end of the day, had some 'parting shot' to say, before an interview was entirely over.*

"It is likely that Jack will want to take his wife back to the UK. That is fine and to be expected. I am sure that you will understand that it would be inappropriate for you to leave with them at this juncture - at least while our investigations are still in progress. You may even be asked to hand over your passport for a time. As for the money, one of my officers will drop by to relieve you of that, I am afraid, at some point prior to you checking out from here. You will of course get a written receipt. Is that entirely OK with you?"

Olga had expected something of the sort. Obviously, no one was going to let them hang on to it.

"Yes that's fine Mr Poska," responded Olga. "I fully understand. I assumed that would be the case."

"So how did it go?" asked Celia anxiously, when Olga arrived back at the room.

"Oh it was fine," replied Olga. "He was pleasant and tried to keep the conversation as informal as possible. There is nothing for *you* to worry about, that's for sure. He said he would not keep you long as he knew that Jack was arriving later. He was good with me but said I would be unable to leave the country for a while. He asked about the money and where it was and I told him it was still here. He said someone would be here to collect it and take it away either today or tomorrow."

"Well that was obviously going to happen wasn't it?" said Celia. "We both knew that. Did you tell him about Angelika - the amount we have given her and what we have promised her?"

"No I didn't, I never brought that up," admitted Olga. "I did not mean to leave that bit out - it's just…"

"Don't worry about it, the whole thing must have been an ordeal for you, however pleasant you say he was. I'll mention it when I see him."

"Alright." said Olga "But you had better go down now, he's waiting for you."

When Celia had left the room, Wesley used the remote to turn his cartoon off, jumped off the bed and stared up at Olga, his little eyes open wide. *He is such a gorgeous little boy,* thought Olga.

"Aunty Olga," the little voice said. "Why are you and Mummy going in and out of the room all the time?"

"Oh, I don't think we are doing it 'all the time' little man, are we? It's just this morning - there is someone we have to talk to downstairs and we don't want to leave a little chap like you all on his own now, do we?"

Wesley thought this over for a moment. He was standing looking up at the lady he called his aunt, as if wondering if he should tell her something. Then a huge smile broke out across his face.

"Auntie Olga," he eventually began. "I have got a secret, a big secret, shall I tell it you?"

"A secret?" said Olga, conspiratorially. "Well you can if you wish but remember, once you tell a secret, it isn't a secret any more then is it?"

Wesley paused to think that through too and then started bouncing up and down.

"Auntie Olga… I've got a Daddy, I've got a Daddy!"

I should have thought of this, mused Olga. *I had assumed that Celia had told him yesterday - after all that's why I was sitting out in the cafe for two hours. I wondered why she never said anything when I got back, but with all the mayhem that ensued, I suppose it's understandable. Then of course, perhaps she did tell him and told him to keep it a secret.*

"A Daddy!" said Olga eventually. "Who told you that?"

"Mummy did! I have got a Daddy and he is coming to see me today. What do you think about that?"

"I think it's wonderful," said Olga, conscious that tears were coming to her eyes and fighting to retain some composure.

"Auntie Angelika's children did not have a Daddy but I have seen people on TV that have a Daddy and I wondered why I did not have one. Because auntie Angelika's children did not have one and I did not know anybody else who did, I thought that perhaps very few people had Daddies."

Olga could not hold it back any more. She was in pieces.

Wesley look at her quizzically and seemed confused.

"Auntie Olga," he said, "why are you crying? Don't you like Daddies? I thought you would be happy because I'm happy. Stop crying, please don't be sad."

She was weeping and he was trying to wrap his little arms around her, to the extent he was able, in an attempt to comfort her.

"I'm alright little man, really I am. I am very very happy. Sometimes grown-ups cry when they are happy, as well as when they are sad."

back to Celia, "is that she is a widow with two children who was controlled by the organisation in a similar way to Olga, though at a much lower level."

"That is essentially correct," said Celia. "She worked for them, mostly looking after my son while I was out on assignments. They hardly gave her enough to put food on the table. She was more a slave than an employee. Keeping her on the breadline ensured that she was kept dependent on them. The fact is, that when Olga and I took the decision to flee, we realised how vulnerable that made her. She would probably be interrogated - and we both knew what that may entail. Olga and I had no doubt that she and her children were in the gravest danger. However, she had nowhere to go, no money to rent and nothing to live on. When we saw the money we realised that a proportion of it could be fairly considered 'back wages'."

Poska raised an eyebrow but let Celia continue.

"The 'long and short' of it," continued Celia, "is that, when we realised she might have somewhere to go, we sent her and the children off with money, sufficient to put her on her feet in the short term and with the promise that we would send her a regular allowance over the next twenty-four months."

"You did did you?" responded Poska, trying hard to keep a smile from creasing his lips. "That was very generous of you. How much money are we talking about with regard to this 'allowance'?"

Celia considered for a moment and then said," including the monthly amounts probably about twenty-five thousand. She would not be living in luxury on that amount but it would hopefully act as a financial buffer. We saw it as money that she had already earned, given how badly she had been treated.

Poska sat thinking for what seemed to Celia like an eternity but probably was no more than a couple of minutes.

"The thing that strikes me," said Poska, "is that I could never have known what was in the parcel in the first place if you and Olga had not mentioned the matter to me, or even if a parcel existed. So it follows that I would not have had the slightest idea that any money had been extracted. It certainly says a lot for you both that you have

181

been so open. You have handled the matter with the highest integrity in fact."

"Whilst I was sitting here, I was doing some quick calculations. First of all, I think you should set aside thirty thousand in total for this lady. Jack has managed his finances very well over the years that I have known him, so though you may not be rich, Celia, you will certainly be what people call 'comfortable.' Your little boy, on the other hand, may need some form of 'care and counselling' as he adjusts to the real world. I suggest you set aside about ten thousand towards that. The work that Olga has done in breaking the organisation in this part of the world has saved the local police force, not to say my department, an incalculable amount. She sees her future as somewhat uncertain at the moment and I can fully understand the reason why. So what I am saying is this Celia, when one of my people come to collect that parcel, I shall tell them to expect around one hundred and fifty thousand euros. Is that clear?"

"It is perfectly clear," said Celia "and thank you very much Mr Poska."

Celia rose and her hand was just on the handle of the door, when Poska called out to her.

"By the way, Celia, does Jack know that he has a son?"

"No, Mr Poska, he will find that out later today."

"I thought not, given I only found out myself this morning. It's wonderful. And Celia, be sure to give him my warmest regards won't you? My best wishes to you both."

"I most certainly will, and thank you again," responded Celia, as she exited the room and made her way back to room 407.

Jack and Celia 2010 May 3rd

"So how do you think we should handle this afternoon Olga?" said Celia to her friend. To be honest with you I don't know whether I am on my head or my heels. I'm terrified Jack will be disappointed. Over three years have passed since he saw me last and I have been locked away for most of that time. Do you think I have got what they call a 'prison pallor'?"

"Of course you haven't, you silly thing," said Olga, coming over to her and offering Celia a hug. "Anyway, you look a million times better than you did when he last saw you."

"How do you mean?" asked Celia.

"Well you were on a stretcher, weren't you? And he thought you were dead."

They both laughed out loud.

"Look, I'll tell you what I think we should do," said Olga.

As we don't know for sure exactly what time Jack is likely to arrive, I will take Wesley out for a walk - not too far and nowhere too busy - perhaps we'll find a toy shop we can look around that will keep his mind occupied - he can't talk about anything now other than seeing his daddy. I think it's driving us both mad isn't it?" she said with a smile. "Then we'll go for a snack somewhere. When Jack arrives, you can spend some time together on your own and then when you want me to appear, phone my mobile. I probably will be no more than fifteen or twenty minutes away. When I get back to our room, I won't use the key card to come in straight away. I will knock first. That way we can manage the surprise."

"That's a great idea, let's do that," said Celia, glad again that Olga was taking control, though also knowing that she had 'some work to do' in that area if she was ever to improve her self confidence.

The call came from reception and after the person in reception had confirmed who she was speaking to said, "There is a Mr Troughton here to see you. Shall I ask him to come up to the room?"

Celia had wondered earlier if she should meet him in the lobby but concluded the room was really the only option, as she was not sure how she would handle her emotions in a public place."

"Yes, that fine," she eventually said and put the receiver down, her heart pounding. She looked across into the mirror for what must have been the tenth time in the last hour. *I'm as good as I am going to get,* she thought to herself with a feint smile.

Less than five minutes later there was a gentle knock on the door and she went forward to open it - and there was Jack - looking virtually the same as she had remembered him. He was wearing a pale green jumper over a cream open-necked shirt, blue chinos and tan shoes.

For a moment they both stood there looking at one another, neither of them speaking. Then Jack walked slowly over to her, circled her in his arms and just held her. Neither of them spoke until Celia broke the silence and through intermittent tears, her head now on his shoulder, sobbed "Jack... Jack.... is it really you?"

They must have spent the best part of two hours talking, laughing and crying. It was a million miles from a regular 'conversation' as they talked over one another excitedly, meandering from subject to subject. Celia becoming increasingly aware of the gaps in her memory and all the time scrabbling to draw elusive recollections together. But it didn't matter. Jack understood and gently strove to put together the missing pieces where he could. He dismissed as unimportant those moments when memories collapsed, like the bubbles that children chase and disappear as soon as they are touched.

Celia looked at her watch. She began to speak and Jack noticed an increased nervousness in her voice. His head went a fraction to one side as she remembered it always had when he was trying to decipher a change in her mood. She watched his eyes scan her face, as he searched for any clue as to what she was thinking.

"Olga has been taking a stroll around town," she eventually said. "She wanted to give us some space and I said I would phone her on her mobile after we had time to catch up a bit. Is it OK if I give her a ring now or..?"

"No, of course that's OK," answered Jack. "It's a long time since I have seen her of course. In fact, I only caught sight of her briefly." Jack was thinking of the blonde woman staring at him through the window of her Audi. I am not sure I will recognise her of course. She had fair hair, that's all I remember I suppose."

"She did have fair, blonde hair, but it's more brown now," said Celia, as she dialled the number, "But that's another story and not for now I think."

It was actually under ten minutes before the knock came on the door marked 407.

Looking across at the door and then bringing her eyes swiftly back to her husband, Celia said, slowly measuring her words, "Jack I have a surprise for you."

Jack met her gaze wondering what she could possibly mean, when he was distracted by the sound of a key card being applied to the lock and so instinctively moved his eyes in that direction. The door opened. Jack saw a woman standing in the half-light of the corridor. In front of her stood a small boy of about three years of age. His little hand was balled into a fist and held against his mouth as he looked uncertainly into the room at the man who now stood beside his mother. He somehow felt a sense of being safe and secure and calm as he saw them standing close together. Then his arm fell way from his face and he rushed forward, his arms outstretched and his little face radiant with joy, pleasure and excitement. "Daddy, Daddy, Daddy it's me - you've found us now, you found Mummy and you found me."

Jack was in shock. He looked to the child, towards Celia and back to the little boy running toward him. Light began to dawn, as he lifted the little boy off his feet and took him into his embrace.

"And so what's your name little man?" Jack asked. "What do they call you then?"

"Wesley, Daddy," a tiny voice said. "My name is Wesley."

There were several gaps in Celia's memory but of one thing she was certain. Never, in all their life together, had she ever seen Jack weep - not even at his father's funeral.

Wesley looked confused as he turned to Celia.

"Mummy, Daddy is crying. Is that sad crying or happy crying, like auntie Olga's?"

Farewell Tallinn

While Celia and Jack had been talking, Olga had visited reception to make a further extension to the booking - just a day or so. For her part, she was now free to return to her own place. In their conversation earlier that day, Poska had assured her she would be safe but to put her mind entirely at ease, he said he would place surveillance personnel in the vicinity of her apartment in the short-term - while she made arrangements to re-locate.

That evening they all had dinner together in the restaurant and Jack was able to listen to Olga's account of Celia's journey. By the end of the evening it was abundantly clear to everyone around the table, that the group would always remain friends.

Jack and Celia had decided that they and Wesley would fly to his place in Manchester and that the three of them would spend a couple of weeks together before embarking on any more 'reunions'. All of them, not just Celia and Wesley, needed to come to terms with the 'new normal'. Not only did Jack have his wife back but he also had the inexpressible delight of knowing that he had a young son. Wesley, so quickly became a 'Daddy's boy', that Celia sometimes needed to check her feelings - not of jealousy but of confusion- given that she and her 'baby' had been locked up in a physical and emotional cocoon ever since he had been born. On the one hand she felt the need to release him to someone else's love and on the other, had to navigate the dynamics of giving herself to her marriage. She was becoming acutely aware that the cross-currents of steering her way through, may result in occasional turbulence - but she had not the slightest doubt in her mind about the outcome. She had the safe harbour of being confident in the love that she and Jack had as a couple and the love that the three of them now had as a family.

Of course, Sarah, Jack's mother had been telephoned within hours of Jack and Celia meeting. She and Aunt Elizabeth were ecstatic. Jack had first thought to make the call as soon as he knew for sure that Celia was alive but knew that the first question he would be asked would be, 'Is she well?' and had decided to leave it until he could answer the question with a greater degree of certainty. When Jack told her that she had a grandson and that Celia had called him Wesley, her reaction had been precisely the same as her son's. Her sister Elizabeth had been sitting across from her as Sarah had been talking and was initially alarmed at seeing Sarah so overcome by emotion, that she had to break the call off saying that she was sorry but would need to call back later. When she had called back it was Celia herself who had answered. Jack had wondered when the call would ever end.

Celia would also chat on the phone with Sue and Damian. Jack had phoned Simon Bellenger, the manager of the Centre in Glasgow. When Jack had come off the phone, he said that Simon had said to mention, that whenever she felt up to it, however many weeks or months later, she must conduct a tour of all the 'Celia Centres' that now existed around the UK. Celia had already learned, through Jack, the nature of the charity and the work that they were all involved in. He had not mentioned until now, however, what the Centres were actually called, and she could hardly take it in.

It would be two months before Jack and Celia would travel to Scotland and Sarah would get to see her grandson for the first time. It was 'love at first sight' when Sarah and Elizabeth met him. Celia's only concern was that he would be shamelessly spoilt. Wesley was proving to be a remarkably resilient little boy. Though still not yet four, he was warm and outgoing, despite his cloistered past, where the only friends he'd had around his own age were Angelika's children.

Celia had been in constant contact with Olga ever since she and Jack had returned to the UK. The thought that her association with the organisation may have meant that she might face prosecution and imprisonment, had hung over her like the Sword of Damocles for months. However, because of the fact that she had been coerced by threats, both to herself and her family, and her subsequent evidence had proved to be crucial in the dismantling of all operations from Estonia to St. Petersburg, she had been granted total immunity. In fact, Poska had been so impressed with her skill-set as an operative, that she was now working for him in his department. She had not been able to tell her closest friend any more than that but Celia was delighted for her and the fact she had seen her mother and was comforted to know she was settled in her new life. Yet all of this news paled into insignificance compared with an email Celia was to receive from Olga in the autumn of that year.

Celia had been entirely baffled by the heading, 'Fifteen centimetres,' until she had read on. It transpired that through conversations Olga had had with people she had met, including even some with Poska, her boss, that her search for God had moved, as Celia had said it should, all the way down from her head to her heart. Her thinking had finally metamorphosed into believing. She had become a Christian. The prayer that her father had prayed over her as he lay dying had been answered. She now had the certainty of knowing that one day she would be reunited with him in heaven.

Elena had become Mrs Bellenger in the Spring of the following year. Celia had never met either of them but was delighted to attend the wedding. It was Jack who was the best man and it was Damian, in the absence of Elena's father, who had led her from the door of the church to the altar to be presented to Simon.

The charity continued to slowly expand both in size and depth. Setting new initiatives in place was relatively easy. Funding them over the medium to long term presented more of a challenge. However, the injection of a bank transfer from an anonymous source in Estonia brought everything back onto an even keel.

It was for the sum of one hundred and fifty thousand euros.

Other books by John Glass

Four
The Best Is Yet To Come
Amrach and the Paraclete
Open Heart, Open Hands
Saying Yes, Saying No
Building Bigger people
Released From The Snare

To order please go to: JohnGlass.co.uk